"I . . . I beg your pardon, Mr. Winter?"

"I'm taking you and Camille home with me," Thornton Winter repeated flatly. "To Charleston."

"You mean," Norah replied guardedly, "for a visit?"

His dark eyes glittered. "What I have in mind, Miss Browne, is much more permanent than a visit, and I see no reason for delay."

Before he had completed his declaration, Norah was shaking her head vigorously. "But that's out of the question."

"It was not a question," he countered. Shadows played on his intriguing face while the lamp flickered and lightning flashed S.O.S. signals against the windows. . . "Obviously you love your baby very much, Miss Browne."

Your baby, he had said?

My baby, she thought.

His implication struck her like the slam of the front screen against the doorfacing. Did Thornton Winter think the baby was hers instead of Hillary's? *Yes, he did,* she thought with dawning certainty. *He actually thought she had borne Lantz a child . . . out of wedlock!*

YVONNE LEHMAN lives in the heart of the Smoky Mountains and has four children. In addition to being an inspirational romance author, she is also the founder of the Blue Ridge Christian Writers' Conference.

Books by Yvonne Lehman

HEARTSONG PRESENTS

HP37—Drums of Shelomoh

Southern Gentleman

Yvonne Lehman

Heartsong Presents

ISBN 1-55748-553-4

SOUTHERN GENTLEMAN

PRINTED IN THE U.S.A.

one

Heavy rain pelted the glass panes. Wind lashed the front screen, threatening to whip it from its hinges. Norah's deep green eyes, darkening with apprehension, darted toward the sound, but it was not the storm that concerned her. She'd been on edge ever since Thornton Winter's telephone call thirty minutes ago. Not only had he known her name and unlisted number, but with a deep-South deliberateness in his voice, he'd asked directions from the airport.

As soon as she hung up, she regretted having told him, then just as quickly reprimanded herself for that attitude. Apparently he felt this visit important enough that he'd flown all the way from California to Florida just to see her.

Car lights flashed across the drapes. Taking a deep breath, Norah attempted to analyze the situation calmly. The man had claimed to be Lantz's brother. Lantz was dead. He'd died yesterday, after a week in the hospital following that awful car accident. Perhaps the grief-stricken man wanted to talk about Lantz and Hillary.

Norah heard the slam of a car door, then the sound of a heavy tread on the walkway along the front of the house. She opened the door to a drenched figure, clutching desperately at his flapping trench coat. With head lowered, he stepped inside.

"This isn't the Florida I expected," came his rueful condemnation, as Norah struggled to close the door against the driving wind.

The height and breadth of the man seemed to fill the small foyer as he stood looking down to unfasten his coat.

"I haven't been here before in April, so I don't really kno-o-o-ow." Her voice wound down like a record at slow speed when he lifted his head, any other words trapped in her throat.

The light striking the left side of his face highlighted in bold relief a jagged pink scar that zigzagged down his cheek to the corner of his mouth. Another cluster of raised scars fanned out from his narrowed left eye, across his temple and into the dark hairline. Try as she might, she could not suppress an involuntary gasp of horror.

She hadn't been curious about Thornton Winter's physical appearance, but now realized she had assumed that he would have the smooth good looks of his brother. On second thought, Lantz had many looks . . . depending upon the role he was playing at the time. This man was not playing a role, she reminded herself, although he did look as if he had stepped straight from the script of a movie, cast as a Gothic villain.

He disengaged his arms from the soaked trench coat and held it at arm's length. "Miss Norah Browne, I assume," he said in a deeply resonant voice in which she detected a decided Southern drawl such as she had noticed in Lantz when he hadn't been trying to rid himself of it.

"Yes, and you're obviously a very wet Thornton Winter," she replied. Forcing her eyes away from his intriguing face, she noticed he was exquisitely dressed in a dark blue suit covering broad shoulders, a white shirt that stretched across an impressively wide chest, and a conservative dark blue tie with a subdued maroon stripe, fastened by a silver-rimmed tie tack encircling what undoubtedly was a ruby stone. His expensive trousers were wet around the bottoms, above black shoes still shiny in spite of the few mud spatters.

Norah was acutely conscious of her faded jeans and dingy white shirt, its tail hanging out, and color flooded her face as she realized he was watching her give him the once-over. Her green eyes flew to his face again where rivulets of rain ran from the thick mop of hair plastered to his forehead, and down along the scar, now purple. A muscle twitched along his jawline. His eyes, glittering like live coals, stopped the apology that formed in her throat.

"Miss Browne," he began, his deep-throated words edged with irritation, "if you have completed your inspection of me, perhaps you will take my wet coat, or tell *me* what I might do with it."

She reached for the coat. "I'm sorry. I wasn't exactly prepared for company."

"I'm not company, Miss Browne," he said abruptly. "I'm Lantz's brother, remember?"

Lantz's brother! The thought smote Thornton like the edge of a steel blade across his heart. He'd tried. Had tried with all his might to be a responsible big brother to Lantz. Had tried to fill the void after their parents died twelve years ago, when Lantz was sixteen, and he, twenty-two. But the void hadn't been filled. Lantz had never seemed to have enough of anything—love, money, attention. He'd packed a lifetime of living in a few short years and, in so doing, had left a string of broken hearts behind him.

This was the first time, and now it would be the last, that Lantz would ever ask Thornton to pick up the pieces of a life burned by Lantz's undisciplined lifestyle.

Thornton had always believed that his brother would return to the traditional Christian faith in which they had both been reared, but he hadn't expected it to be on Lantz's deathbed, while he was still a young man with so much of life yet untasted. In a halting voice, Lantz had told Thornton what he would do differently, if he could do it all over again.

Unfortunately, it was too late. Lantz couldn't do it over again.

But Thornton was still alive and well, in spite of having been met head-on by the raging elements pounding the Florida coast, not to mention the intense scrutiny of Lantz's most recent "indiscretion."

Thornton had always known that Lantz attracted beautiful, glamorous, even older, sophisticated women, so he was not surprised by this one's face, whose features were as lovely as a magnolia blossom and whose unusually expressive eyes were as green as spring in Charleston. But he had not expected her to be so young. And at the moment, she appeared disheveled and somewhat disoriented. Well, he supposed that was to be expected under the circumstances. What caused him some pain, however, was her unabashed repulsion as she stared at his face.

"You'll like her," Lantz had said only hours before his death. "The two of you have a lot in common."

Thornton hadn't said so at the time, of course, but Lantz's leftovers weren't at all his type. Still, one so young, so apparently helpless would doubtless welcome the proposition he was about to make. But welcome it or not, of one thing he was sure—he knew what had to be done, and Miss Norah Browne wasn't about to stop him!

It was still hard for Norah to believe that this man and Lantz were brothers. Physically, she recognized little family resemblance, and their personalities were exact opposites. Lantz had exuded charm, a smile for everyone, and an easy-going magnetism that drew people to him. Lantz would have already extended his hand, at the very least, or more likely would have pulled a person to him for a friendly hug.

Not this one! So formal and aloof was he that Norah had the impression he'd rather not be here. Then why was he? Shouldn't he be seeing about his brother's affairs?

The screen door slammed against the doorcasing just as a chilling thought thudded into her brain. Surely he didn't think there was anything *here* for him to handle!

Suddenly, she felt the cold wetness of the coat on her arm.

A shiver ran through her. Instinct warned that this man had not come for a purely social visit, nor merely to express sympathy.

Did he know about Camille? If Lantz hadn't mentioned her, then . . . .

"Have a seat in the living room," Norah said lightly, making an instant decision not to provide any unsolicited information.

Winter's glance followed hers toward the living room, in plain view from the small foyer. It was dimly lighted by the glow of a TV, where players romped across the silent screen, and a lamp that flickered precariously as the wind whipped the electrical lines outside as if turning a jump rope.

Norah watched him peer inside and view the room with apparent disdain—much the way he'd looked at her. She had no choice but to find out what was on his mind. The first thing, however, was to rid herself of the dripping coat.

She walked down the hallway and glanced uncertainly over her shoulder toward the living room. Then, stealthily, she tiptoed to Camille's doorway, peeked in, observed the baby sleeping peacefully, and quietly closed the door. What Thornton Winter didn't know already, he didn't need to know.

While hanging the coat over the shower curtain rod in the bathroom, Norah admitted to herself the reason she had not been able to keep her gaze from lingering on Thornton Winter's scar. The truth was she'd always been more intrigued by a gnarled tree limb than by a perfect rosebud. Her insatiable curiosity, along with an innate sense of caring, had led her to decide upon a career that probed the innermost depths of a person.

Thornton Winter's marred face had certainly aroused her curiosity. *Whatever had happened to cause such disfigurement? An accident? An act of violence?*

Judging from the man's dark, brooding expression,

however, he was not the type to bare his soul, and she wasn't about to ask! For just as Lantz's brother did not possess the younger man's pretty-boy features, instinct warned that he also lacked Lantz's good nature.

Turning to look in the mirror, Norah touched the thick coil of braided hair, secured with hairpins on top of her head. *It looks like a pile of orange marmalade*, she thought with a sigh of disgust. Dark circles shadowed her weary green eyes that stared out of her face, pale now except for the sprinkling of freckles across the bridge of her nose. The old joke she'd heard umpteen times—"You must have swallowed a dollar and it came out in pennies, ha ha!"—had never been a consolation. And now she could readily see that the strain of the past week had taken its toll on her. Too bad. It was too late for makeup.

A spot on her shirt caught her eye. Camille's cereal! That must have happened earlier in the evening. She hadn't noticed at the time, and a change of clothing now would only call attention to it. Since Thornton Winter's call, Norah had had time only to settle the baby after her bottle around 10 o'clock. No wonder he had looked at her as if she had a contagious disease.

Hearing a movement, Norah jerked her head toward the bathroom doorway and gasped to see him standing there. What a picture she must make, with a washcloth wrapped around one finger and a wet streak down the front of her shirt. His dark eyes lingered on the spot for a moment before he raised them to meet her gaze.

"I seem to be dripping all over my suit and the carpet," he said, with a definite edge in his voice. "Could you possibly spare a towel?"

"Of course," Norah replied nervously, aware of the man staring at her and the tumultuous activity outside the bathroom window. She knew, without a doubt, which of them made her more uncomfortable.

After taking a towel from the linen closet, Norah handed it to him. He wiped his face, and for an instant the towel covered the left side of his face. *Why, he's beautiful!* came her surprising reaction as she stared at the unblemished side, smooth except for the dark shadow of a heavy beard. He didn't seem quite so foreboding now. That is, until his eye met hers. And in that moment his glance held such contempt that she felt she had been accused and found guilty.

Turning sideways to avoid any physical contact, Norah scuttled past him and escaped up the hallway, reprimanding herself for being on the defensive. Yet, analyzing the situation, how could she be otherwise? She hadn't even known Thornton Winter existed until half an hour ago. Lantz had never talked to her about family. If he and his alleged brother were close, then why hadn't Lantz mentioned him before?

The lights blinked off, the TV gulped, and Norah almost stopped breathing. Then everything came to life again. Standing inside the doorway of the living room, Norah tried to convince herself that she was in no danger.

But sudden fear gripped her heart and her pulse raced madly when he strode up beside her, their bodies almost touching. She could feel the body heat emanating from him, strangely prickling the icy gooseflesh on her arm. And when she lifted her inquiring face to his, she was again spellbound. The scarred tissue at his eye seemed to be stitched, and it stretched the eyelid into a narrowed slit, from which a dark orb glittered ominously.

The uneasy realization dawned that she had allowed a strange man into the house. He could be anyone at all! Only her resolve to protect a helpless baby held at bay an invading sense of panic. "I would like to see your identification," she demanded, with more courage than she felt.

A glare of indignation swept his features, deepening the color

of the scar to a purple streak, and she feared he would refuse.
What she would do next, she had no idea.

Then, without taking his eyes from hers, he reached into his
breast pocket and withdrew a thin wallet. "My calling card.
Credit cards. Driver's license." He flipped from one plastic
covering to another, then held it out to her. "Rarely does one
resemble such photos, as you know, but the vital statistics are
there."

Norah wondered whether his resentment was spawned by
her impertinent request or by the photo itself. It was the im-
age of an incredibly handsome man—stormy dark eyes, a
straight nose, wide sensuous lips that curled over perfect
teeth—without a trace of a scar. The wound must have been
inflicted fairly recently. The dark wavy hair in the photo-
graph was neatly brushed, while the man who stood before
her, his dark curls in damp disarray, now showed touches of
gray at his temples, presenting a certain air of distinction along
with his villainous charisma.

"I thought you could be a reporter," Norah murmured, moist-
ening her suddenly dry lips with the tip of her tongue. Her
long lashes veiled the humiliation in her green eyes as she
returned the wallet. Attempting to ease the tension with an
attempt at humor, she asked coyly, "Would you like to see *my*
identification?"

He surprised her. "I would, indeed. You see, the purpose of
my visit is to see my niece."

Norah stepped back and gripped the doorjamb. He knew!
It was perfectly natural, she tried telling herself, that he would
leave his dead brother's side, fly to Florida late at night in the
most unsightly weather of the season, just to see a baby he'd
never seen. Perfectly natural! Then why was her heart batter-
ing against her chest like the wind against the windows?

"I . . . she . . . she's sleeping."

With calm deliberation, he said, "I can wait," and swept

past her into the living room.

Norah reached out and grasped the sleeve of his suitcoat. "No! Wait. . . .," she tried to protest, then heaved a sigh of resignation. He *was* Camille's uncle. He had every right to see her.

She had to remember that they were both under tremendous strain. At least, she had been forced to accept Hillary's instant death. But there was no way of knowing what Thornton Winter might have experienced during the past week, while his brother hovered between living and dying. She would be cruel to deny him his right to see Camille, if for no other reason than to set his mind at ease about her welfare. And then he would be on his way.

"Come with me." Norah retreated down the hallway, with Thornton Winter a few steps behind. She opened the door, and the sweet scent of baby powder greeted them from the nursery. A Mickey Mouse nightlight glowed near the crib.

He lifted his hand to prevent Norah's turning on the lamp atop the chest of drawers.

"It's all right," she assured him quietly, switching on the lamp, illuminating the colored balloons held aloft by a smiling clown.

"I don't think a child should be reared in silence and darkness," Norah explained softly. "As long as the noise and light are within normal limits, they don't disturb her."

He cast her a speculative glance before his gaze swept the room, taking in the Babyland decor and the pink carpet. Then he turned his attention to the white crib.

The faint glow of light revealed the baby, whose tiny pink lips parted with each quiet breath. Camille lay on her stomach, her head turned to the side, her plump little cheek facing them. A halo of golden-red ringlets curled all over her head.

Norah's heart went out to the beautiful baby, who someday would have to know the tragedy that had occurred.

"What do you call her?" Thornton Winter asked finally, his voice surprisingly tender.

"Camille," Norah replied.

"Camille," he repeated and nodded slightly, as if he approved. "Sounds like a flower, or a song."

Norah smiled as she and Mr. Winter gazed at the child.

"Lantz's child," Thornton murmured. The words caught in his throat.

A quick glance at his face revealed that he was deep in thought. Norah was suddenly aware that this was Lantz's house. Lantz's baby. Lantz's brother. Feeling a chill, Norah reached over and tucked the pink blanket closer to Camille's chin, then switched off the lamp.

They returned to the living room and stood inside the doorway. "She's adorable," Thornton acknowledged, as if he could not quite believe it.

Norah agreed, adding lightly, "Even though she's very demanding. Those middle-of-the-night snacks, you know." She laughed weakly.

She had hoped for some sign of congeniality. But he didn't laugh, not even a tiny smile, and Norah flushed beneath his poignant stare. Then his eyes traveled toward the windows, rattling their protest against the torrential wind and rain.

"Would you like coffee?" Norah asked. "Before you go back out in that?" She glanced toward the windows.

He didn't reply. Norah looked up at him. Perhaps he hadn't heard her. Then ebony eyes stared down into her face. "Yes, please."

They were sitting across from each other at the bar separating the kitchen-dining area when Thornton asked, "Are you an actress, Miss Browne?"

"Actress?" Norah repeated, staring into her milky coffee. She wasn't at all the glamorous, exciting type like Hillary. Perhaps Thornton Winter's perception had been dimmed in his grief over his brother's death. Or perhaps he thought her a bit-part actress, hanging onto her sister's skirttails. "No, I'm not an actress," she answered finally.

"How did you meet Lantz?"

"Through my sister Hillary, of course."

"Hillary Caine is your sister?" he blurted. Coffee spilled from his uplifted cup. His scar reddened.

Norah could not readily grasp his bewilderment. Apparently Thornton Winter knew as little about her as she did about him.

"Caine was Hillary's professional name," Norah explained. "She was Hillary Browne."

"I'm sorry," he said, spreading his hands. "Had I known Hillary Caine was your sister, I would have immediately expressed my condolences."

He took a napkin from the holder on the bar and wiped up the spots of coffee. "Lantz could say very little, and when he did, it was in broken sentences. Until the end," he said, pausing, "I had no idea he had a child. Under the circumstances I couldn't very well ask for details."

Glancing around, he found a trash can for the soggy napkin, then returned to pick up his cup and drink from it, while his dark eyes probed hers from over the rim.

Norah brushed back a stray piece of red hair and fidgeted on the bar stool. *Strange*, she thought. His words expressed one sentiment, while his eyes, for some reason, seemed to convey quite another. He should be satisfied. He had seen for himself that the baby was well cared for, content.

The situation was painful for her, too, but she realized the therapeutic value in sharing a crisis with another person. She recognized the element of shock after Hillary's death, then the tension of waiting to hear if Lantz would survive. "You never met my sister?"

"No, never. Of course, I've heard of Hillary Caine

professionally and have seen her on the screen. She was a very beautiful, talented young woman."

The sympathy in his voice surprised Norah when he added quietly, "Your burden of grief is much greater than I realized."

Norah lowered the cup to the saucer with a trembling hand. Somehow she had kept pretending that Lantz and Hillary were in California on assignment, and would be back any day now. At the same time, she knew she would have to come to grips with losing Lantz as a friend, Hillary as a sister. Her greater concern, however, had to be for Camille.

"It's Camille that makes all this bearable," Norah said softly, "in spite of the pain that comes from losing loved ones." Norah bit her lip in an effort to hold back her tears.

It wasn't sympathy, but a note of accusation that Norah detected in Thornton's reply. "I should think that's what a baby would mean to any married couple."

Norah drew in her breath. Maybe there was more Thornton hadn't known! But with his loss so fresh, she didn't want to risk compounding his grief. She'd have to be very gentle, make sure the time was right before explaining that Hillary and Lantz had been in love and had had a child outside of marriage. With their careers at stake, they hadn't thought public acknowledgment of the baby would be good for either of them at the present time. Hillary had been a child star, and was just becoming accepted as mature talent. And Lantz was already established as one of Hollywood's most exciting celebrity bachelors.

In her own code of ethics, Norah believed that love and marriage should precede the birth of a child, but it wouldn't change anything to discuss it with Thornton Winter. It was late. She was tired. He had expressed his sympathy and had seen his niece. Perhaps he would finish his coffee and leave.

"How did you find out about me, Mr. Winter?" she asked, curious.

His expression grew pensive. "I've been with Lantz all week. Only near the end was he able to speak coherently. He seemed to be clinging to life only to tell me about his child. But he did know that Miss Caine was killed in the accident and blamed himself."

"He shouldn't have," Norah replied, looking down at her hands, clasped together on the bar.

The periodic updates on the horrible accident had played over and over on the television news. They flashed through her mind now. The late-night party. The heavy rains. The mudslide blocking the highway. Lantz hadn't seen the mud and rocks in time and had skidded down an embankment.

"It was unavoidable," Norah said finally. She saw the restrained grief in his eyes and felt an uncanny desire to reach out and put a comforting hand on his arm. However, one glance at his forbidding countenance put the skids on that impulse.

"In any event," Thornton said quietly, "Lantz had a picture of Camille in his wallet. Your name and phone number were on the back." He hesitated, then added almost kindly, "You were in his last thoughts. His last words, in fact, were about you."

That surprised Norah. "Wh—what did he say?" she stammered.

"After he asked me to take care of Camille, he said, 'Norah makes a great little mother.'"

That vote of confidence from Lantz caused Norah's eyes to mist over. "I've tried," she said in a whisper. "It takes more time than I could ever have imagined. But, Mr. Winter, the most natural impulse in the world is loving that little baby."

"You're a very, um . . . tolerant young woman," he said, "not minding that Lantz was in California with your sister, while you were clear across the country."

"If I minded, I wouldn't be here, Mr. Winter," Norah said, stating the obvious. "Their careers were very important to

Lantz and Hillary."

"A career is more important than a baby?" came his scathing remark. Norah suspected that there was something other than grief eating away at Thornton Winter.

"Parents don't necessarily give up their jobs when a baby is born," Norah said tightly. "Some jobs just happen to take a parent across the country instead of downtown."

"You miss my point altogether, Miss Browne." His voice was cool and remote.

"Just what *is* your point, Mr. Winter?"

He downed his coffee, pushed the cup aside, and stood. "Perhaps we'd be more comfortable in the living room," he said, sounding for all the world like the bearer of bad tidings.

But what could be worse than the current situation?

Her emotions were raw—that's all, she told herself. Keeping them under control for Camille's sake had been difficult. Now to have Thornton Winter here in some unexplainable capacity gnawed at her. Determined not to break down in front of him, she quickly slipped from the stool, then tossed over her shoulder, "I'll check on Camille and be right back."

She looked in on the baby, still sleeping peacefully, and thought about Thornton Winter's words. What had he meant about Lantz asking *him* to take care of Camille? He obviously intended some kind of financial assistance, since he had acknowledged that Norah "made a good mother."

Norah took a deep breath, reminding herself to be wary of Thornton Winter's questions. And of her own answers. In times of emotional stress, one didn't always think rationally.

Upon entering the living room and walking across the beige carpet, her attention was immediately drawn to Thornton, already seated on the couch, at the end nearest the picture window. The contrast between the two brothers again struck her forcefully. Lantz's gaze had been touchingly transparent and open, while Thornton's eyes continually searched hers, as if he were harboring some deep secret and suspected her of one, too.

Norah had barely seated herself in the overstuffed chair when he asked with slow deliberation, "What are your plans now, Miss Browne?"

"Plans?" Norah echoed, her thoughts whirling. She wished she could simply lean her head back, close her eyes, and sleep off her overwhelming exhaustion. "So much depended upon whether or not Lantz lived. But, no, I haven't made any definite plans yet. It was only yesterday that . . ."

"Yes, yes, of course," Thornton interrupted. After a moment, he asked, "Did you attend your sister's funeral?"

She could see no harm in answering that question. "My parents felt it would be adverse publicity for the reporters to find out about Camille. I don't think anyone knows about her except me, my parents," she hesitated, then added tersely, "and you."

He caught the inflection in her voice, confirming what he suspected. She resented him. But that was of no consequence. His mission here was not to establish a friendship, but to assume his responsibility. "Do you plan to take the baby to your parents?"

"They . . . travel a lot," she began, and told him that her father was a character actor who was in constant demand. Her mother had spent years in the makeup department of a major studio before she had quit her job to concentrate on reliving her acting dreams through her daughters. Hillary had gladly followed in their footsteps, but Norah had not been in the least interested.

"They've looked forward to this time in their lives when they would not be bound to any particular place." Noticing the slight narrowing of his eyes, she wondered if that sounded callous, and hastened to explain. "My parents came here when Camille was born, of course, and spent several days.

And we've talked on the phone since the accident. They're willing to help if necessary, but I know grandparenting is the role they want to play and should play."

The mention of grandparenting presented a memory that tugged at Norah's heart. She saw herself as a carefree child, running along the beach, startling sandpipers, secure beneath the watchful eyes and protective arms of her grandparents. They were gone now, but from them she'd learned about the frailty of human arms and the strength derived from the awesome presence of God, through His Spirit dwelling within the believer. Consequently, she'd found a kind of confidence and fulfillment in being herself, that she never felt on stage, with human hands applauding her portrayal of a character.

"You said you're not an actress, Miss Browne," Thornton was saying, bringing her errant thoughts back into line. "May I ask . . ." He cleared his throat, "just what is your line of work?"

Noticing his hesitation, Norah wondered if he were having qualms about this obvious cross-examination. On second thought, Thornton Winter did not give the impression that he was ever uncertain about anything. Probably, he was only trying to discover if she could care for Camille adequately. That would be a natural concern. Particularly for one who had been asked, by his dying brother, to look out for his child.

"I expect to find a job in some phase of psychological work," she went on. "I earned my Bachelor's Degree in psychology last spring, worked at a health clinic in southern California during the summer, and began work on my Master's in the fall."

Thornton grimaced. His brother had obviously taken advantage of this schoolgirl, had halted her career plans and gotten her pregnant, had settled her in Florida, and had then gallivanted across California with her glamorous sister. And to make matters worse, this girl didn't even seem to know she'd been wronged.

He took a deep breath rather than chance spouting some unappreciated remarks about morality. The young woman was looking at him as if she were afraid he might hit something. And well he might! This latest escapade topped anything Lantz had ever done! Her voice trembled slightly as she continued, "Then . . . I came here."

"Because of the baby, I assume," he said.

Norah's "Yes" was barely out of her mouth when Thornton rushed on, "Then you have no ties or obligations to a job or persons either in California or Florida?"

"Only to Camille," Norah replied firmly.

Ah, he's convinced of my devotion, Norah thought when a trace of triumph flashed in Thornton Winter's eyes. But his very next words astounded her. Surely she had misunderstood him. No way on Florida's drenched earth would she consider doing what he was asking!

"I . . . I beg your pardon, Mr. Winter?"

two

"I'm taking you and Camille home with me," Thornton Winter repeated flatly. "To Charleston."

"You mean," Norah began guardedly, "for a visit?"

His dark eyes glittered. "What I have in mind, Miss Browne, is much more permanent than a visit, and I see no reason for delay."

Before he had completed his declaration, Norah was shaking her head vigorously. "But that's out of the question."

"It was not a question," he countered. Shadows played on his intriguing face while the lamp flickered and lightning flashed S.O.S. signals against the windows.

"I have other plans," Norah said quickly, trying to control her inner panic.

"You just told me that you have no plans. But I *do*!" Before she had a chance to recover from that announcement, he shocked her speechless with his next words. "Obviously, you love your baby very much, Miss Browne."

Your baby, he had said?

My baby! she thought.

His implication struck her like the slam of the front screen against the doorfacing. Did Thornton Winter think the baby was hers instead of Hillary's? *Yes, he did*, she thought, with dawning certainty. *He actually thought she had borne Lantz a child . . . out of wedlock!*

"You're . . ." she croaked, bracing her hands on the chair arms and planting her feet on the floor, in the act of standing.

"Don't faint on me, Miss Browne!" he warned, rushing to assist her.

To escape the threat in his eyes, Norah slunk back into the chair, her initial shock turning to outrage. Color now leapt into cheeks that had paled considerably. Defiance and determination stung her eyes. No way would she faint and leave that helpless child in his clutches!

She flinched as his hand came up, then was aware of his fingers, surprisingly gentle, as they touched her shoulder. "Have you been eating properly, Miss Browne?"

"Eating?" Norah returned. Chagrin washed over her like the storm over the Florida landscape. Feeding herself had not been a priority in the past twenty-four hours.

"Sit still," he demanded, then moved away.

A moment later he was back, holding a glass of milk. "Here, drink this."

Norah took it, her hands trembling.

Thornton returned to the couch, but she could feel his eyes on her as she drank. After the first taste, her stomach became aware of its absence of nourishment and grumbled. She finished the milk, sipping slowly while she collected her thoughts.

"Mr. Winter," she said finally, studying the glass. "I'm afraid you have some very mistaken ideas about me."

"Never mind that," he said brusquely. "You don't have to explain to me, Miss Browne. You're hardly more than a child yourself. I admire your determination, but there would be nothing wrong with your allowing me to relieve you of this responsibility."

Norah's mouth dropped open. When she finally found her voice, it rose shrilly. "I don't want to be relieved of it!" she protested. "Why would you think such a thing?"

"Well, you're young, and single, and," he paused then had the audacity to appear slightly embarrassed before adding, "and apparently quite . . . uh, impetuous . . . to have gotten into such a predicament." He lifted his hand to halt any protest. "Never mind," he said before she could reply, "some things are better left unsaid. We must try to put aside our emotions, as difficult as that might be, and concentrate on that child in the other room."

Norah had the strange feeling that she had just been labeled "damaged goods" and consigned to the nearest garbage dump.

Just as she was about to set him straight by blurting out her true relationship to Camille, something unexpected happened. A mothering instinct surfaced, as surely as if she had given birth to that child. As Camille's aunt, she didn't stand a chance against Thornton Winter. But as her mother . . .

"What did Lantz tell you?" she asked, strangely serene. His humiliating perception of her was something she could endure if it meant protecting an innocent child. A baby needed gentleness and love more than she needed financial security from a domineering, judgmental uncle.

Thornton hesitated before answering. "A dying man's words are focused on eternity, Miss Browne, rather than on things of this world. However, after I discovered Camille's picture, with your name and number on the back, I asked him if he had married you. He shook his head 'no.' That was right before he asked me to take care of Camille." Thornton leaned forward, his disapproval evident in the frown on his face. "Did he refuse to marry you, Miss Browne? Or was that *your* decision?"

Norah now welcomed this misconception. It gave her the confidence to deal with this overbearing man. "I am single by choice," she replied with a defiant lift of her chin.

His glare of disdain gave her the feeling that a storm raged inside him, proportionate to the one outside. She delighted in his discomfort. It served him right!

She had a feeling that Thornton Winter had auditioned her for a role in traditional morality, and she hadn't landed the part. Well, she knew she could play the role of Camille's mother convincingly. After all, the baby's welfare was much more important than Thornton Winter's opinion of her.

He exhaled audibly and sank back against the couch. Lantz must have been hallucinating to think that this loose young woman and he had anything in common. Apparently, she was one of those star-struck groupies who fall for celebrities without giving a thought to the consequences. But what excuse hadd Lantz had—at age twenty-eight?

And how could his brother have believed that he would *like* her? He couldn't even communicate with her. All she had done so far was flash those green eyes and dart at him like a wary cat showing her claws, getting her back up at every word, when all he was trying to do was to offer her a chance at a decent life. Obviously, she hadn't an inkling as to what was good for her or the baby. For a so-called well-educated person, she hadn't a grain of common sense. She was being totally unreasonable.

Unless . . . and a thought struck him. Could she be holding out for . . . blackmail? With the help of an unscrupulous attorney, she could present that innocent child as heir to the famous Lantz Winter estate.

Thornton's determination increased. He wasn't about to let this fiery young woman out of his sight until he knew what made her tick.

Norah reminded herself that both Lantz and Hillary had entrusted the care of their child to her. This had now been confirmed by Lantz, who in his dying breath had acknowledged his approval of her. So she hoped the quivering she felt inside was not evident in her voice as she stated as firmly as she could manage, "We don't want your help, Mr. Winter. Thanks, but no thanks."

"That doesn't change a thing," he retorted. "What you want, Miss Browne, does not affect what I believe is my responsibility. My niece is going with me," he replied as calmly as if he had said, "I believe the storm is subsiding."

Norah didn't budge. "Your concern is appreciated, Mr. Winter. However, I will decide what is best for me. And for Camille."

"You're in no position to think rationally," he insisted with infuriating calm. "So I'm here to do it for you." The only indication that he felt any emotion whatsoever was the reddening of his scar.

Norah's green eyes flashed. "Really, Mr. Winter? Do you plan to resort to force?" Her voice rose to a dangerous pitch.

"I wouldn't call it force," he argued. "May I remind you, Miss Browne, that I'm not trying to take something *from* you. I'm making you an offer."

Norah couldn't chance it. If he discovered she was only the child's aunt, there would be no hope of keeping Camille. She shook her head. "I don't want to go to Charleston with you, Mr. Winter."

"Why are you resisting my offer?" he asked suddenly.

Why? The answer washed over her in a wave of panic. She'd lost her grandparents. Then Roman. Now Hillary and Lantz. The fear of losing yet another close to her trembled through her veins. To cover the shaking of her hands, she set her glass on the coffee table. She mustn't think of herself . . . only Camille.

"Camille needs *me*, Mr. Winter. But as her uncle, you're certainly entitled to visit her occasionally." Another thought occurred to her, and she used it to fuel her argument. "After all, the child's name is Browne, not Winter."

"Be sensible, Miss Browne," he implored, leaning forward again and placing his arms on his knees. "I don't want to make threats. I'm simply trying to do what is best for everyone concerned. Let's look at the facts: You have no visible means of support, you do not want to live with your parents, and you have a child to raise."

"I'll get a job."

He quirked a brow. "Enough to provide for a decent place to live? A babysitter? Even the basic necessities are costly these days."

Norah tried not to think of the few hundred dollars in her checking account, compared with the extensive list of supplies a baby would need. "What she needs most, Mr. Winter, is emotional security and love."

"Camille will have all that in Charleston—a stable home, a loving family, people who will teach her Christian values."

As if I have none! Norah thought resentfully. "And how would your wife feel about your bringing Camille and someone like . . . me . . . home with you?"

A glimmer of triumph shone in his eyes. "I have no wife."

Norah felt an unexpected surge of elation tingling through her, and she tried to ignore the images flashing across her brain and threatening to alter her heartbeat. She'd spent many years backstage, waiting for her walk-on part, while her family rehearsed. Meanwhile, she had occupied her time by reading and had become fascinated, not with the white knight on his white horse, but with the villain, brandishing his sword, his black cape flying. In her dreams, she saw someone darkly handsome coming to her rescue, someone who was not a villain at all, but her hero!

She shook off these mesmerizing thoughts. This kind of fantasy could be dangerous. Sometimes the main character turned out to be a true rogue. Right now, she should keep her mind on what was best for Camille.

Norah cleared her throat. "That presents a problem then, Mr. Winter," she began. "For Camille's sake, I must think of my reputation. Despite what you might think, you need to understand that I'm not in the habit of allowing strange men to support me."

"I had no thought of propositioning you, Miss Browne," he replied as if nothing could be further from his mind. "Frankly,

I was thinking of Lantz's child."

She sighed wearily and closed her eyes. Of course he wasn't propositioning her. A man like Thornton Winter would have women falling at his feet, just as Lantz had always had. But she needn't worry about this one. He did not seem to like her at all. In fact, he was downright hostile.

She knew his patience was at an end. So was hers! She rose from the chair and walked to the picture window. Pushing aside the drapes, she looked out. The wind had quieted, and the rain was coming down in a steady drizzle.

Glancing over her shoulder, she saw that Thornton Winter was sitting calmly, his legs crossed, one hand resting against his bent knee. The scarred side of his face was toward her. She wondered what had happened. *Perhaps,* she thought indignantly, *he had backed someone into a corner, as he was doing to her, and he . . . or she . . . had come out fighting.*

In the half-light, she was conscious of the man's appearance. He was immaculately groomed and expensively attired, all the way down to his shoes and socks. His hands were large and strong, yet delicately tapered, and the nails were well cared for. His dark, tailored suit fit perfectly across the broad expanse of his shoulders and skimmed a slender waist. He had not even loosened his well-knotted tie during his entire visit. While his dress and bearing were that of a southern aristocrat, Norah had the distinct impression that here was a man who was accustomed to having his own way.

At least, he seemed determined to take Camille. Norah knew she could do nothing legally, and she was no match for him physically. Nor had her psychology courses prepared her to tackle a personal problem of this magnitude. But one thing she knew. There was no way she would give up that baby!

She would just have to use her wits. She took a seat in a chair opposite him, thinking furiously.

"I assure you, Miss Browne," he went on quietly, "in

Charleston, the baby's every need will be met. I have hired help. I will engage a nurse. . . ."

"A nurse?" Norah felt as if her voice had become a perpetual squeak. "You think a nurse can replace . . ." Yes! She'd say it, "a . . . a mother?"

"Obviously, you're not thinking straight, Miss . . ."

"Because I don't agree with you?" she snapped.

"On this issue, yes. We are going to Charleston," he insisted.

"You seem to think I have no choice in the matter."

Thornton leaned forward. There was no trace of amusement in his voice now. "Certainly you have a choice." His tone sent a chill down her spine. "I'm taking Camille to Charleston. You may come peacefully . . ." He paused for effect—"or not."

Norah winced. She could mention the authorities, but if he called her bluff, that could lead to a court fight and she couldn't risk that.

She glanced at the wall clock. It was nearing midnight. *Let Thornton Winter have the last word,* she was thinking. He obviously was not playing games, but was determined to take Lantz's child to Charleston, whether or not she went along. She would simply have to agree . . . for now.

Norah took a ragged breath and closed her eyes. "All right, Mr. Winter," she said quietly, as if resigned to the fact, "Camille and I will go to Charleston with you."

During the ensuing silence Norah opened her eyes, aware that she was being observed. She fastened her gaze on the scuffed toes of her tennis shoes.

"Your cooperation is appreciated, Miss Browne," he said, after a long moment. "I sincerely believe you will not regret your decision."

Norah stood, hoping he could not see the fluttering of her heart. As soon as he left, she would consider what she should do. She still had the option of stealing away during the night and driving Camille to her parents' home in California. "Then it's settled, isn't it, Mr. Winter? I'll get your coat so you can leave, and we can both try for a good night's sleep."

He stood, his eyes gleaming with some kind of sinister delight as they met hers. A sardonic smile touched the corners of his lips as if he knew what she'd been thinking. "Don't bother with the coat," he drawled, his words thick and slow as molasses. "Just show me where I might sleep."

three

Sleep?!

Norah would not be able to close her eyes with Thornton Winter lying in the darkened guest room with the door open. Norah suspected that he lay on the bed fully clothed, waiting to pounce should she make a suspicious move.

Midnight in Florida meant that it was eight o'clock in California. She could call her parents. But what would she say? *Drop all your plans . . . interrupt your career . . . rescue me and Camille?*

"Rescue you? From what?" they would ask.

Norah pondered what she would say. *Camille's uncle is here, intent upon taking over Lantz's responsibility for her. He's insisting we go to his home where there is financial security, loving family, Christian values. . . .*

Somehow, she couldn't imagine her parents replying, "In that case, run for your life!"

She drifted into a restless sleep, still fretting over the fact that she was helpless in the face of Thornton Winter's demands.

When her eyes opened, she focused on the gray light rimming the window. It couldn't be morning! But it was!

She had slept. Guiltily, she admitted to herself that it must have been because someone else was in the house to listen for the baby. Norah had fed Camille sometime in the wee hours of the night and then again just as the faint rays of a gloomy dawn invaded the house.

A car door slammed, soon followed by the hum of an electric razor, then the cascade of the shower—reassuring, masculine sounds. Yet Norah could not contain a shiver of apprehension at the prospect of the future this man might be planning for his niece.

"You can trust me," she promised Camille, while settling the baby in her crib. "I won't ever leave you."

When she entered the hallway, Thornton stepped out of the bathroom. He was wearing the trousers to his suit of the day before, but the white shirt looked fresh.

"We have a big day ahead of us," he said exuberantly, and Norah wondered if he were always so chipper this early in the morning. "But the first order of the day is breakfast." He rubbed his hands together in anticipation.

Norah flushed with anger. He looked perfectly rested and fresh, while she felt frazzled, bedraggled, and heavy-headed from having slept the sleep of the exhausted. Taking care of a baby was one thing, but she had no intention of becoming this man's slave, too!

"There's cereal in the kitchen," she said shortly, her indignation bringing her fully awake.

Thornton gave a snort and disappeared down the hallway.

Norah showered, slipped into blue jeans, tennis shoes, and a T-shirt. She wrapped a thick towel around her dripping auburn curls and tucked the corners in at the nape of her neck. Suddenly the most marvelous aroma assailed her nostrils. Food! Realizing she was hungry, she hurried to the kitchen.

Taking note of the two places set at the bar, Norah immediately felt a stab of guilt. She shouldn't have been so hasty in her judgment. But she quickly dismissed her concern. After all, Thornton Winter had taken it upon himself to lay claim to his brother's belongings, including his child. He might as well realize that a few other responsibilities went along with the privilege.

Norah unwrapped the towel, allowing her hair to tumble below her shoulders.

Thornton eyed the tangle of red-gold curls. "No wonder

you have such a fiery temper," he observed, walking over to the bar, skillet and spatula in hand. With the dexterity born of practice, he deftly lifted an omelet onto the plate in front of her.

"It's not the hair," she informed him rather self-consciously, having detected a trace of admiration in his gaze, if not in his words. It was not uncommon to hear compliments on the glorious mane that waved naturally and hung to her waist when brushed out. But at the moment, she felt it was about as attractive as limp strands of wet spaghetti noodles.

After toweling her hair dry, Norah used her fingers to coax the ringlets away from her face. When Thornton returned to the bar with a second omelet for himself, his continued scrutiny unnerved her, and she responded automatically to his terse command. "Sit down and eat everything on your plate. We have much ahead of us, and you'll need your strength."

She grasped the fork almost as soon as the backside of her jeans made contact with the bar stool. The omelet was a simple mixture of eggs, cheese, and milk, but her green eyes narrowed as the golden-yellow concoction teased her palate and aroused a response from the pit of her stomach.

Norah was halfway through with her breakfast before she realized that she had been lost in her own thoughts and that the only sounds had been the occasional muffled noise of her chewing and the slight scrapes of butter knife against crunchy toast.

Looking up, her eyes met Thornton's across the bar. She felt certain he had been staring at her for some time. Warmth crept into her cheeks. She sat a little straighter, aware of how she must look, hovering over her plate as if she hadn't eaten in days.

"And you suggested only cereal?" he drawled, amused.

She refused to succumb to his charming grin. "I guess I was a little hungry," she confessed, finding him even more handsome and younger than he had appeared the night before. Was she warped to find a scar so intriguing?

The light caught the glint of a gold chain around his neck, nestled against his chest beneath the open collar of his shirt. She quickly averted her eyes from the mat of dark curly hair, forcing herself to remember that Thornton Winter had come to claim her treasure—baby Camille. Of course, his chest would be hairy. Wasn't Bluebeard's? And dangling from that chain around his neck was probably a skull and crossbones!

Perhaps Mr. Winter seemed like pleasant company because she'd had a few hours sleep and had eaten her first hot meal in a week.

"What kind of car do you have?" he asked, jolting her thoughts back to the stark realities of the moment.

Avoiding his eyes, which were a deep tranquil blue this morning, she described her car—a small car, standard gear shift, six years old. "It was a high school graduation present from Mom and Dad."

"I think we'd better take the rented one," he decided.

Norah bristled. "What's wrong with my car?"

His steely eyes bore into hers. "Your car would barely hold the three of us, Miss Browne," he tried to explain reasonably. "And we have your personal belongings to take, as well as Camille's."

Norah prodded the remains of her omelet with her fork. The car had represented her independence. In it, she had driven to the beach when she wanted to be alone. She had driven from California to Florida when Hillary had needed her. Now, Thornton Winter was saying she would have to leave it behind.

"I—I'll need my car," Norah protested, her nerves feeling more jangled by the moment.

Obviously irritated, Thornton set down the steaming cup of coffee he had just poured. "If you need a car, you may drive one of mine until I can move yours to Charleston."

Norah had already discovered the futility of arguing with him. Besides, the little Rabbit had become more and more temperamental, often having to be coaxed into doing her bidding. But she wouldn't give in so easily. "Isn't it rather expensive to drive a rented car all the way to Charleston?" she persisted.

"When we consider the possibility of breaking down somewhere along the way, my ineptness with gears on the highway, and your having to care for an infant, I think all the comfort we can get is recommended. However . . ." He shrugged his broad shoulders, his back to her at the sink, "if you want to pay for it. . . ."

"I do not!" Norah retorted angrily. "It's *your* idea. I'm perfectly willing to take my own car."

A sly grin touched his lips as he turned to observe her. He slowly wiped his hands, threw the towel over his shoulder, then ambled over to the bar. With his face uncomfortably close to hers, he repeated her words, "Perfectly willing . . . to go with me, Norah?" He suspected she was not as reluctant as she pretended. Nor was she as naive. But even if she really wanted nothing for herself, surely she would not deny that baby her birthright as the child of Lantz Winter.

Before Norah could object, he continued in a deep singsong tone, "You don't really want to fight with me, now do you, pretty Norah with the wild, curly hair?"

His words were pleasantly reminiscent of a song her grandfather used to sing, something about Jeannie with the light brown hair. . . .

Ever since their first encounter, Norah had recognized within herself the fight or flight syndrome, accompanied by the dawning realization that she really did not want to fight with Thornton Winter. Now, almost hypnotized by his disturbing nearness, her gaze lingered on the fan of scars at the corner of his eye, then moved down the streak along the side of his face.

"It . . . bothers you?" he asked, touching the purple welt with a tentative finger, then quickly added, "Never mind. Of course it does." He moved away abruptly.

"Please . . . I," she began, aware that she had offended him.

"Don't bother with apologies or explanations," he ground out. "I've heard enough of them to last a lifetime." His dark eyes were fathomless pools of shadow, and a scowl touched the lips that had come so close to hers. "Let's just say you caught me at a weak moment. But frankly, I don't know whether to shake you or console you."

Norah's heart pounded furiously. She wanted to pour out the truth to him, but he shrugged as if it were inconsequential and turned to carry the dishes to the sink. Was it possible that this self-assured man was the slightest bit vulnerable to her? Or was it just part of his ploy to further subdue and control her? And how could she ever know with this deception between them? He thought she had been his brother's lover. There would come a day when he would call her a liar. She must tell him the truth.

"Mr. Winter," she began slowly. She felt he was listening, though he did not turn from his chore. "I . . . need to tell you something."

Thornton submerged the plate in the sudsy water and scrubbed it over and over. The wetness reminded him of the liquid emotion that had threatened to scald his eyes during the night, while he stared at the dark ceiling and heard the steady rain beating against the roof. He had feared he might drown in his own grief as he replayed the memory of his dying brother and his last request. Suddenly thrust upon him was the life-long responsibility of rearing a child. With that had also come the question of how to deal with that child's mother.

It would be simpler to say he'd tried and failed, and leave her to her own devices. But, earlier, while Norah was taking her shower, he'd gone to the nursery to look in on the baby. Camille had started to fret and, fearing Norah's recriminations, he'd picked her up.

She had stopped crying almost immediately, turning her cornflower blue gaze on him with such innocence and purity that his heart melted. She seemed to be reading his mind, extracting a silent promise from him. And in that moment he made a firm decision. He would not abandon his brother's child.

He'd even felt grateful that Miss Norah Browne had produced this miraculous little girl. Camille would never feel her daddy's arms around her again, but her uncle would do his best to make up for that.

But first, there was Norah herself!

Thornton knew he had been hard on her, and he felt a momentary twinge of remorse. But how was one expected to handle a woman who didn't know what was best for her? He had found Norah Browne to be extremely perceptive and dedicated to the welfare of her child. But she was utterly exasperating as well! Still, in her defense, he had to admit that she was very young, relatively alone in the world, and still grieving for her sister . . . and her lover. To compound the problem, she appeared frightened of what Thornton might do, and he resolved to be kinder . . . gentler with her.

Now he'd gone too far in the other direction. In his attempt to blunt his own pain and the burden of his new responsibilities, he'd allowed himself to become vulnerable. Well, it was inexcusable. He simply couldn't handle any more complications right now.

Now this impossible young woman wanted to tell him something. He hoped it was not another revelation . . . that she was a jewel thief on the side! At the moment, he felt about as fragile as the plate he was washing. With the slightest jolt, it could break apart. He sighed. He'd have to hear her out. Better get it over with.

Thornton wiped his hands and walked over to the bar. "What is it now?"

Norah took in the stubborn stance, the hands folded over his chest. Basic Psychology told her that this signaled a defensive posture. Nor did his dark scowl and one quizzically lifted eyebrow encourage her to continue.

Determined, she plunged in anyway. "I'd rather not begin this . . . arrangement . . . between us with dishonesty. We need to try to get along. For Camille's sake."

"I agree," he concurred.

Norah drew in a breath. She was not actress enough to pull off this deception any longer, but she couldn't find the words, so she used a diversionary tactic. "You and I need to have at least a mutual understanding that Camille's needs come first, and that we should put any animosity behind us."

Thornton, who was still stinging from his own raw emotions and his perception that she found his looks unbearable, lashed out with a tart reply. "Then maybe I'd just better leave you here and take Camille."

Norah's eyes flashed with green fire. "You try that, Mr. Winter, and I will let this story out to the press and the police and whomever else is necessary! I've taken care of that child since the day she was born, three months now. You may have more money than I, but that's all. You certainly can't be a mother to her!"

He threw back his head and laughed. "Quite a spitfire, aren't you, Miss Browne? Comes with the hair, I suppose."

She cocked her head and glared up at him. "I'm whatever I have to be."

His disarming grin caught Norah off guard, and she felt herself thawing. But it would never do for Thornton Winter to know he had her on an emotional roller coaster ride. Still, his next words made her wonder.

"In spite of your protests, Miss Browne," he said, still

grinning into her eyes, "I believe you're looking forward to the prospect ahead as much as I." She held her breath when he rose from the bar stool and towered over her for a moment.

But before she could summon up a scathing rejoinder, he was issuing orders again. "But now, we've work to do. I realize you're a modern woman, Miss Browne. But since I've done the cooking and cleaning up, maybe you could do your own packing. Take only the essentials. Pack what is to be shipped later. Label everything. We have several hours drive ahead of us, so please, let's have no further delays."

Stung by the implication that she had staged the delay, she darted him a murderous look, then twirled on the bar stool and jumped lightly to her feet. Rushing from the kitchen, she went into her bedroom to throw some things into her suitcases. Poor Camille. Why couldn't the child have a nice, kind, old uncle rather than this arrogant, overbearing tyrant?

While she packed, Thornton made some telephone calls. Snatches of his end of the conversation revealed his finesse in handling business affairs, including funeral arrangements for Lantz in Charleston. Then there were hurried references to "house, dock, weather," after which he phoned the electric and telephone companies to see about disconnecting the service. He had thought of everything. For that, she was grateful.

&

The gray late-afternoon sky pressed ominously low as Norah and Thornton left the house she had called home during the past several months. She climbed into the back seat of the rented new Buick, next to Camille's wicker car bed.

Thornton grimaced as drops of rain struck his face, then he slid under the steering wheel and started the engine. "When you need to stop, just let me know," he tossed over his shoulder.

After a curt nod, Norah glanced at Camille, who was waving her little arms and making loud cooing sounds. *Babies are so trusting,* she thought. The poor little thing had no idea where she was or where they were taking her. Didn't care, as long as she was warm and dry and her tummy was full.

Norah let out a long sigh and looked back at the house as they pulled away. Only a week ago, she had been a loving aunt, filling in for absentee parents. And then the accident had changed everything. Now a man she had never met had appeared to complicate things even further. But Thornton Winter was right. In spite of everything, she could begin to feel an inexplicable stir of adventure. What might be awaiting her in Charleston?

When Camille fell asleep, Thornton persuaded Norah to sit up front. "You'll be more comfortable," he said.

Norah doubted that but slid into the plush front seat and buckled her seat belt. "How much longer until we get to Charleston?"

"Several hours until we reach the city limits. Then we have to drive through the city, cross the Cooper River Bridge, and out to Seabreeze Island."

"Island?"

Thornton glanced at her quizzically. "Didn't Lantz tell you anything?"

Norah could reply honestly. "Nothing about his family . . . or home."

Thornton sighed and nodded. "He wanted to break free of all that. Make it on his own without help from any of us."

"Tell me about your family."

"We have a younger brother and an aunt."

"Oh!" Then it would not be just the three of them. "They live with you?" Norah asked expectantly.

He glanced over at her before turning his attention back to the road. "No. Chris is in school at The Citadel, and Aunt Tess has her own place."

Norah swallowed hard. How could Thornton Winter expect her to live in a house with him? How could he possibly think that was a better arrangement than the one Lantz and Hillary had? But that was not her worry. How to get Camille away from him was the important issue. As soon as possible, she would go to her parents' home, then work toward legal adoption.

For now, she'd play the role of acquiescent mother.

"Suppose they aren't in favor of two new family members?"

He glanced at her, lifted his eyebrows, and replied blandly, "In my house, Miss Browne, I make the decisions."

Norah turned her head and looked out the side window. That's exactly what she was afraid of.

four

Hours later, the sky yawned and the sun presented itself in the guise of a huge yellow ball, reaching out to tantalize the water with its golden rays. Norah caught her breath while Thornton drove onto a glimmering structure of burnished steel that rose high and higher, from one crisscrossed peak to another, like a giant web of strength. The intricate design lifted them and cradled them high above the ships, looking like toys, floating on the water hundreds of feet below. Awestruck, Norah watched as the bridge narrowed out ahead as if their journey was taking them straight into the sunset.

Only after they had traveled for miles and had begun their descent, did the clouds clamp shut like giant jaws, swallowing the evening sun. Norah looked over her shoulder at the impressive structure, then ahead, as the world faded to muted shades of gray.

"The Cooper River Bridge," Thornton said at last, having given her time to absorb the spectacle that had been known to frighten many first-time tourists. Strangely enough, Norah did not seem in the least intimidated. Her eyes were shining!

"Seeing the strength and power of the steel bridge always reminds me of the power of God," Thornton observed with a glance in her direction. "How His strength carries us over the rough seas of life."

Norah turned to look out her window. Normally, she could appreciate such an analogy and draw courage from it. But the words struck her heart fearfully. Thornton Winter was demanding enough on his own. Suppose he decided the Lord also wanted him to bring up Camille . . . without her help?

42

Surely, God would not let that happen. He knew Camille needed a woman in her life.

With the approaching night, drivers turned on their headlights, and lamps winked on in homes as they drove through a small town. On the outskirts, Thornton followed a narrow road until he reached a private dock, drove out onto a ferry, and spoke with a uniformed security guard.

Only a few minutes later, the ferry reached the opposite shore and bumped to a stop. Thornton lifted a hand in farewell and drove the Buick onto a paved road that twisted across a bed of sand like a giant snake. On the way, the car lights raked a couple of Victorian beach cottages, planted among a copse of scraggly pines and green-brown grasses struggling for survival in the rocky soil, and spotlighted stately green-gold palms towering high above great barren stretches of sand. Norah rolled down the window to catch the cooling ocean breeze on her face and breathe in the pungent salt air.

Suddenly, Norah saw the house looming ahead. The camera was ready to roll. Soon she would have to play her part.

The road straightened, ending in front of a modern structure with bright light spilling out from glass walls and windows. Low-growing palmettos, flowering shrubs, and lush greenery surrounded the concrete drive that forked at the house, built on a slight incline.

The structure, built of glass and wood, gave her the impression of a bird in flight, its body stretched forth, its wings spread out on either side. The head was a balcony above the front entrance, topped with a peaked roof.

Thornton took the left curve, drove beyond the recessed front entrance, past the far wing and into a lighted carport when he braked to a stop beside a dune buggy. As soon as he switched off the engine, a slightly stooped, gray-haired man appeared from the back of the house, joined by a white-haired woman in a light blue housedress who stepped from the doorway.

Thornton introduced the couple as Mr. and Mrs. Manchester, and Norah noticed that the man eyed Camille curiously when she was lifted from her car bed. In the next moment, he was helping Thornton remove the bags from the trunk.

"Could I take the baby?" Mrs. Manchester asked softly.

Norah placed Camille in her arms, retrieved the diaper bag and her own purse from the car, and followed the trim woman into the house and along the corridor to the second door on the right.

Mrs. Manchester crossed the ash-colored carpet to a crib and gently lay Camille on her stomach. The baby stirred restlessly, then popped her thumb in her mouth and went back to sleep.

"So precious," Mrs. Manchester said, turning toward Norah. "When Henry told me that Thornton asked him to have a baby crib ready, I thought he must have heard him wrong." A question formed in her eyes. "He said it was Lantz's baby. . . ."

Norah nodded and watched Mrs. Manchester's eyes grow misty. "Lantz was so special. . . ."

"Yes, and the crib is fine. Please call me Norah."

"And I'm Eloise," the older woman replied. She gestured toward Mr. Manchester who was bringing in a couple of bags. "This is my husband Henry. Now, you must be tired after all you've been through. Let me help you get your things unpacked. And I have grandbabies, so I know all about changing diapers, too."

Norah put the diaper bag on the king-sized bed. "Have you known the Winters long?" she asked.

Eloise smiled. "The Winter boys are like my own." She explained that she had been their nursemaid when they were young, and Henry the landscaper for the estate. They were retired now, helping out when Thornton needed them. She and her husband lived in one of the Victorian cottages Norah had seen on the way to the house. "Living on this island is like living in paradise . . . thanks to Thornton," she added fondly.

Then Thornton must own the cottages too, Norah surmised. She unzipped the bag and took out a diaper, smiling at the ease with which Eloise changed Camille, turned her again on her stomach, and put the pacifier in the baby's mouth.

While Mrs. Manchester disposed of the wet diaper, Norah walked around the room, trailing a finger across the pale wood furniture, noting the white walls hung with pastel seascapes. Rose draperies could be drawn to separate the bedroom from a sitting area. Here a couch upholstered in a floral design with a matching chair and a window seat padded in pink, composed an intimate grouping. Outside the windows that stretched across the entire front wall, could be seen low palmetto palms bordering a grassy incline. And beyond the rolling landscape Norah glimpsed the ocean, and a familiar excitement stirred in her veins.

"Tell me what needs to be done, and I'll help," Eloise offered when Norah stepped back into the bedroom.

"Camille will need some formula," she said, casting a skeptical eye at the boxes Henry had brought into the room, "but I'll have to find it first."

"Then I'll run along and see about supper." Eloise gave her directions for finding the kitchen and slipped out, closing the door softly behind her.

Seeing that Camille was still sleeping peacefully, Norah went into the carpeted bathroom, splashed her face with cold water, and tucked in a few strands of hair that had escaped the braid coiled on top of her head. As she looked into the lighted mirror above the vanity, she was surprised to see that some of the strain of the past week had lifted.

In the next instant she had accounted for it. For the first time in weeks, she was having real conversations with other human beings. Someone else had driven her here. Another had changed Camille's diaper. She smiled, feeling as if she'd had a mini-vacation.

After finding the box of bottles and formula, Norah left the bedroom door open and headed for the kitchen. On the way she walked through what appeared to be a game room, situated somewhere in the central part of the house.

Her attention was immediately drawn to an outside area, beyond the glass doors and windows, where light reflected off a huge swimming pool onto the wooden deck surrounding it. At the far end of the pool, shrubs and palm fronds spread out like the tail feathers of a bird.

Hearing male voices and the sound of approaching footsteps on the deck, Norah hurried past a white wicker couch set against the wall, over which two large flower prints were centered. A conversational grouping of wicker chairs with lush padding, squatted at opposite ends of the glass wall. A pool table waited invitingly, balls and cuesticks arranged for play.

Separating the game room from the kitchen was a long bar flanked by six wooden stools on either side. Just beyond, the kitchen was a study in contrasts. Pristine cabinets sparkled against pale yellow walls. Gleaming white tile covered the floor, and a round table sat under exposed cedar beams.

"It's a wonderful house, Eloise," Norah said, walking into the kitchen. "Straight out of the pages of *Architectural Digest*."

Eloise smiled and took the box of formula from her. "Oh, it's been featured there," she said proudly. "Thornton designed and built it, you know."

While Norah was trying to absorb that remark, Eloise opened the box and took out a can of formula and began reading the directions on the back. "Just add water?" she questioned.

"Boiled water," Norah replied. "Then we pour a day's supply in the little plastic bags."

"When I think of all the baby bottles I've sterilized!" Eloise said, shaking her head.

The two women had just finished preparing enough bottles of formula to last Camille through several feedings when Thornton opened the glass doors, stepped inside the game room, and walked toward the kitchen.

Norah had turned away to put the bottles in the refrigerator and, out of the corner of her eye, noticed Thornton picking up the bottle that Camille would soon be demanding.

"I had hoped for something a little more substantial, Eloise," he chided good-naturedly. "It's been hours since I've had any solid food."

What a difference a tone of voice makes, Norah thought. Had Thornton made that remark to her, it would have sounded cryptic, condemnatory.

Eloise laughed. "Now, Thornton, I'll have something for you in a few minutes."

"Good," he said. "In the meantime, I can give Norah a tour of the house."

Norah! Since when had he decided to use her given name? Norah wondered. Was it because he didn't know what else to call her since bringing Lantz's baby home? Eloise must be terribly curious.

Norah wiped her hands on a towel and followed Thornton through an archway and into the dining room. A crystal chandelier, suspended from the ceiling, illuminated the entire area. A massive wooden table, capable of seating twelve, presided over the room. Slate-gray carpeting covered the floor, and the walls were paneled in wood-stained platinum. The outside wall was entirely of glass with the exception of a few feet of paneling ending in a ledge lined with a jungle of leafy plants.

A see-through fireplace, set into a wall of coral rock, separated the dining area and living room.

"Eloise said you designed this house. I'm impressed," Norah admitted.

He smiled in acknowledgment and walked over to one of the tomato-red couches that faced the fireplace. Inside the grouping was a low, glass-topped table resting on a silvery shag rug.

"You're an architect?" she asked, glancing around the room, spare and uncluttered, yet elegant in its concept. Heavy white drapes hung at each side of the glass walls, framing a window seat padded in red. Matching fern stands with long graceful legs relieved the stark lines of the room.

"Something like that," Thornton replied as they reached the spacious front foyer dividing the two wings of the house. From here a staircase wound its way to the second floor where a white railing overlooked the open foyer.

"My rooms are upstairs," Thornton said, following her gaze. "The best view of the ocean is from my deck. Feel free to make use of it any time."

Norah lifted her eyes to his for the first time since they had begun the tour. "Mr. Winter," she began, wanting him to understand that no matter how beautiful his home might be, she resented being forced to come here, nor did she intend the visit to be permanent.

"Couldn't we drop the formality?" he asked. "We're family now." A softness appeared in the deep blue eyes. "We have a little relative in common, you know."

At the same time Norah was aware of Thornton Winter's appeal, like a rose of intricate design whose uniqueness draws and mesmerizes while disguising the thorns so near the petals' velvety folds.

Yes, they had a little relative in common, but if Thornton Winter took over, where would that leave Norah? He was willing to accept her, if necessary, but he had made it abundantly clear that any informality between them was nothing personal. Everything was done for Camille's sake. If this continued and Thornton Winter had his way, Norah fumed inwardly, she would become nothing more than a glorified babysitter.

At the moment, the name *Thornton* didn't come naturally to her lips. "The important thing is that Camille's needs are met," she said quietly. "That she feels safe and loved."

He prevented her turning away by grasping her shoulders with both hands. "What you've done with my little niece impresses me . . ." His touch was warm and strong as he added, "very much."

The angry redness of the scar deepened, but she knew she dare not stare. Accepting a compliment from him was difficult. She could feel it cracking the defenses she must keep intact against him. But how to do that and still behave like a decent human being, she wasn't sure. "I've done the best I could," she murmured.

"I know. But now you have others to help. You no longer have to bear the responsibility alone."

Against her will, Norah felt herself faltering, tempted by his offer of security. How she longed to be comforted, to be reassured that everything would work out. She couldn't be sure of that, however, and she mustn't allow the silent tears to surface. She was not at all sure of Thornton Winter . . . or what his offers meant.

Dropping his hands, Thornton blushed hotly, and the scar turned a livid purple. She could feel him withdrawing, and once again he was his aloof self, and his peremptory gesture toward the foyer told Norah the tour had ended.

When the doors behind them swung closed, Norah felt as if much of the tension were left behind in those coolly beautiful rooms, for stepping into the kitchen was like stepping into sunshine. Eloise's cheerful smile reflected the butter yellow of the draperies and was as welcome as the savory aromas that assaulted Norah's senses and stirred the hunger in her stomach.

Places for two were set at the small round table in the corner, and Thornton held out a chair for Norah and motioned her into it. She obeyed, then breathed a silent prayer for help as the bewildering drama continued to unfold.

Thornton took his seat across from her, spending an inordinate amount of time adjusting his napkin in his lap. In those few moments, Norah reminded herself that she had two overwhelming advantages over him. One was her unyielding love for the baby. The other was Thornton's belief that she was Camille's natural mother.

"It smells wonderful, Eloise," Norah told her when she brought over the steaming bowls of rice and shrimp creole.

"Thank you. But you need to know I'm not much of a cook. That's Hilda's department."

Before Norah could ask who Hilda was, Thornton laughed. "You're fishing for compliments, Eloise," he teased, grinning boyishly. With a wrench of her heart, Norah realized how pleasant and appealing he could be—to everyone but herself.

Eloise brought over hot biscuits and butter, then poured a glass of iced tea for each of them.

Norah savored a bite of the creole, then looked toward Eloise. "Never say you're not a cook."

Eloise laughed appreciatively. "Well, we won't tell Hilda. You just enjoy your meal, and I'll check on the baby."

"You're fortunate to have found someone so competent," Norah said sincerely after the woman had left. "Normally, I wouldn't let someone take over like that. But I think I'm just beginning to feel the strain of it all. . . ." She paused, prodding the creole with a shaky fork.

"Caring for another human being twenty-four hours a day is more than anyone should have to handle alone, Norah, even under ideal circumstances," he said sympathetically. "Now eat up. You need your strength."

Norah lifted another forkful to her mouth and gazed out

toward the game room's sliding doors. Everything was dark now. Henry must have turned out the outside lights in preparation for the night. She wondered again if she, Camille, and Thornton would be the only ones occupying this house, since apparently Eloise and Henry lived in one of the cottages. And where did Hilda, the cook, fit into the picture?

"Mr. . . ." she began, after swallowing a sip of tea. His first name still wouldn't come. She began again. "Mr. Winter, your home is beautiful. And the design is perfect for the ocean setting."

"Yes?" He looked up from buttering a biscuit, obviously intent on hearing what she had to say.

She felt a little flustered. She was no expert, but she did know what she liked. "When I caught my first glimpse of this place, I thought it looked like a huge seagull, with its wings spread, ready to fly out over the sea."

He squinted in approval. "That's exactly what I had in mind when I began the design. I wanted to blend the structure with its surroundings, to capture the light, airy essence of sea and sky, and offer a sense of power, yet freedom. Not everyone sees that without the explanation first."

At his look of admiration, Norah cautioned herself about putting too much stock in this rare moment of camaraderie. It wouldn't last!

"But frankly," he went on, "I'm surprised that you would allow me to think you're pleased with anything I've done."

"I recognize superior talent when I see it," she said with a lift of her chin. "That has nothing at all to do with our present . . . uh . . . dilemma." She thought for a moment, struggling to find a way to learn more about him without prying. "I love everything about this house. But it is quite different from what I would have expected."

"And what might that have been?"

She chose her words carefully, not wishing to insult him on

the brink of their first decent conversation. "I guess I expected something . . . more traditional."

Norah didn't understand the slight furrow that appeared between his brows. She watched him swallow a bite of food, then wipe his lips on the cloth napkin, his intense eyes scrutinizing her. "This is not my permanent residence, Norah," he confessed. "It's only the beach house."

Norah's eyes widened, and he continued. "The reason I didn't take you and Camille to my home is because this is the season when visitors tour the historic homes in the area. Mine is on the list. Since there are only two weeks left, I didn't think I should cancel."

"I understand," Norah assured him quickly, for he seemed so ill at ease. "Frankly, a beach setting is more appealing to me anyway."

He moaned, looking slightly amused. "Don't say that too loudly in these parts, Norah. People literally come from around the world to see these historic old homes you have so casually dismissed. Do you have any inkling of all the time, effort, and expense that goes into restoration?"

"So you renovate old homes?"

He grimaced again. "You make it sound so ordinary, but . . . yes."

It figured, Norah thought to herself. He was exactly like one of those old houses—stuffy, rigid, unyielding, standing staunchly through the years, oblivious to the changes taking place around it. "I suppose I don't really know how to appreciate history," she confessed.

"You're young enough to learn," he said matter of factly. "Charleston is one of our nation's oldest and most majestic cities. And . . ."

His lecture was interrupted by the ringing of the telephone at the end of the bar. As he walked over to answer it, Norah wondered if he planned to take on *her* education as well as

Camille's. The audacity of the man!

Still fuming, she nibbled at her food while Thornton talked to the caller, his end of the conversation sounding fragmented and disjointed. "No, you stay with Aunt Tess. . . . Madelyn? Yes, I can pick her up. What time does her flight get in?" He paused to listen. Then, "No, I won't be home tonight. Tell Aunt Tess I'll see you both in the morning. Take care, Chris."

He hung up, then rejoined her at the table. "I don't suppose you know about Chris, either?"

She shook her head.

"You and Lantz didn't talk much, did you?"

Norah choked on her tea, and her cheeks flushed scarlet.

Thornton stifled a smile of amusement and began to explain. "My younger brother is about your age—nineteen, almost twenty."

"I'm twenty-three," Norah informed him emphatically. Her announcement resulted only in the lift of a sable brow. The gesture spoke volumes. Apparently she was still little more than a child to him.

Refolding his napkin, he rose. "I have to leave and won't be back tonight. I'll ask Henry and Eloise to stay here, in the bedroom next to yours. You and Camille will be quite safe."

She wasn't ready to say good night, not just yet. "Thornton . . ." There, she had said it! "You've told me about everyone except Madelyn. Who is she?"

Leaning on the back of his chair, he said wearily, "Madelyn is a long-time friend of the family. She's flying in from Paris for the memorial service tomorrow." There was an imperceptible pause. "Have you decided whether you'll be attending?"

"I won't be going," she said in a small voice, expecting his disapproval. She rose and walked over to the sliding glass doors and looked out into the dark night.

He came to stand beside her. "That's probably a wise decision," he said, to her surprise. "The family doesn't know about

Camille, and I need to find the right time to tell them. So, you just take tomorrow to relax. The family will come here for Sunday dinner. In the meantime, Eloise will be here with you and anything you need is as near as the telephone."

Norah studied their reflection in the glass pane of the window—the shabby girl in jeans and the distinguished-looking mature man. A strange feeling crept over her. He'd given her a tour of the house as if she were a guest. He'd fed her at his table as if she were a friend. But in reality she wasn't even a poor relation; she was a prisoner here.

"Suppose I want to go into Charleston? Will a car be available to me as you promised in Florida?" she tested him.

She felt the tension, even before he spoke. "You're welcome to come and go as you please. There's a dune buggy in the carport and cars at the dock. Henry could bring one in for you. However . . ." Norah held her breath, feeling the blood drain from her face. She knew what he was going to say before the words were out of his mouth. "However," he repeated firmly, "Camille should stay right here."

"And suppose I tried to take her with me?" she asked, her gaze rising to meet his.

His reply was uttered slowly and distinctly, so there could be no mistaking his meaning. "Don't even try. You wouldn't get very far."

"I see!" Norah snapped. "My presence here is tolerated, but not accepted. You want Camille here, but not me. You would prefer that I leave, wouldn't you, Mr. Winter?"

Thornton didn't deign to answer her question, but stepped so close that he could feel the hot anger emanating from her body. He tilted her chin with one finger, forcing her eyes to meet his. "The family will be coming for Sunday dinner," he said, "and I hope by that time you will have your hair out of that ridiculous braid."

She glared at him, speechless.

Suddenly his countenance darkened, and he dropped his finger and stepped back, digging both hands into his pants pockets. "About your leaving, Norah," he began grimly and she could hear the weariness in his voice, "please don't. Not tonight anyway. How on earth would I deal with that tiny baby in there?" He gestured toward the bedroom. "Especially now that Madelyn is coming."

Norah couldn't resist his unaccustomed tone of entreaty. She had not the faintest idea why Madelyn was so important to him, but she could understand the terrible strain he was under. And since she had no intention of abandoning her sister's child, she said firmly, "Camille and I will expect you on Sunday."

He appeared satisfied with her reply. "I'd like to say goodnight to Camille before I go. Do you suppose we could call a truce long enough to do that?"

Norah opened her mouth to protest, but he turned and strode toward the bedroom door without waiting for her reply. She followed him.

Eloise had emptied most of the boxes and stored the contents in drawers. As Thornton entered, she looked up from the open suitcase on the bed. "The baby is ready for her bottle now. I'll go and get it," she said and left the room.

Norah walked over to the crib, picked Camille up, and cuddled the baby in her arms.

Thornton put out his finger to the child, and she grasped it firmly, her eyes intent on his face. Norah watched as the big man took in Camille's baby antics, his expression mellowing. Could he possibly feel as Norah herself did? Sometimes, caught up in the miracle of this new little life, she could temporarily forget all about her troubles, the problems facing her.

"Do you know," he asked, incredulous, "I may need this little girl as much as she needs me." Norah could only stare into his eyes, so close to her own, as a puzzled expression settled on his face. "Now how do I get my finger back?"

"Oh!" Norah exclaimed, startled out of her reverie, and managed to help him unwind the tiny fist from his finger, whereupon Camille expressed her outrage.

Thornton stepped back, casting a skeptical glance at the baby. "Has a temper like her mother," he observed. He glanced at Norah. "I'll find Eloise and the bottle," he promised.

Why am I smiling? Norah asked herself, staring at the doorway through which Thornton Winter had disappeared. What she had felt for him in those few tender moments was far from hostility. But somehow this glimpse of his softer side was far more frightening than the overbearing tyrant. That Thornton Winter she could fight. But what defense did one have against a vulnerable man who admitted his need of a little child in his life?

five

Sitting in the shade of several scraggly palms, Norah gazed beyond the warm sand to the white-tipped waves disappearing into the blue horizon. She had sat in this same spot yesterday, breathing in the moisture-filled air and shivering from the cool mist on her body. She had needed that time alone to collect her thoughts and begin to recover from her recent ordeal.

Yesterday, after Henry and Eloise had returned from Lantz's memorial service, Norah had raced down to the sandy beach and plunged into the icy water, allowing herself the luxury of pouring out her grief, mingling her tears with the vast ocean. The deaths of Lantz and Hillary had brought vivid reminders of her grandparents and had revived old feelings for Roman, who had met his untimely end less than a year ago.

Later, exhausted, she had lifted her face toward the overcast sky, uttering a prayerful tribute to the memory of Lantz and Hillary and renewing her own vow concerning Camille's welfare.

The clouds had disappeared overnight and now the southern sun warmed the gentle spring breezes and dried the sand. Norah's eyes fell upon her lengthening shadow. It must be four or five o'clock, just enough time to dress for dinner. With a sigh, she left the secluded stretch of beach that had become her sanctuary, her shield against the world, a world that must now be faced.

Approaching the beach house, Norah concentrated on the palms, the blooming azaleas and other flowering shrubs coming into view. A smile touched her lips as she recalled how, in the early morning, moisture-like beads of dew, like diamonds, had glittered on fragile blossoms and outlined the spiny leaves.

Seeing a white Mercedes and a light-blue Jaguar parked in front of the house, she stopped abruptly. They were early, and she couldn't afford to be seen like this, she thought, looking down at her swimsuit-clad body! She could scarcely cover herself with the single small towel she had carried with her to the beach. "What on earth can I do?" she said aloud.

Deciding to try to make it into the house undetected, Norah went through the carport. After sneaking to the corner, she peeked around. One quick glance revealed several figures gathered on the deck. Before she could duck out of sight, Thornton's hawk-like eyes had found her. "Norah!" he called.

Norah could only squint against the unexpected assault of late-afternoon sun. She guessed she had no choice but to walk forward and face them.

Stopping several feet away, she held the gritty towel in front of her. "I'm sorry," she murmured. With her right hand, she pushed back the stiff strands of hair that had come loose from her "ridiculous" braid. "I thought you would not be coming until later."

Thornton strode toward her. The silver streaking the jet-black hair at his temples enhanced his charcoal-gray suit and darker patterned tie against a stark white shirt. His scar had deepened in color, a sure sign that he was disturbed.

"Please forgive us," he said with a trace of sarcasm. "I phoned that we were on our way, but you weren't available to receive that call. I trust we haven't come at an inopportune time."

Norah felt herself flush scarlet under his penetrating gaze, painfully conscious of her scanty attire, but feeling even more emotionally exposed. A helplessness stole over her as the irony of his words brought home the fact that this was his house, and he and his family could appear at any time they pleased.

"Oh, Thornton," a well-modulated voice scolded, "do stop jesting with that lovely girl and tell us who she is."

Norah, grateful for the intrusion, saw a tall, silvery-haired woman stroll over to stand beside Thornton. She looked lovely in an elegant gray suit, a pink-patterned blouse reflecting her rosy complexion.

"This is Norah, Aunt Tess. Latessia Spearman, my father's sister," he said affectionately.

The woman smiled warmly. "Oh, don't mind him, Norah. Everyone calls me Aunt Tess."

"And this is my brother Chris," Thornton said, when a lanky young man stepped from the shade of the cedar overhead.

Taking Norah's hand, he exclaimed, "Well, if you aren't the prettiest thing to come out of that ocean in a long time!" Chris' eyes danced merrily, reminding her of Lantz.

"Thanks, Chris." She leaned toward him, confiding in a whisper, "I needed that."

Thornton urged her forward, toward a woman sitting well back in the shadows. "Madelyn McCalla, Norah Browne."

Norah held out her hand and Madelyn took it halfheartedly. Her chilling gaze traveled through Norah and beyond. "How do you do," she said in a stilted voice, then she looked down at her delicately tapered fingers, nails buffed to a high gloss.

Norah found Madelyn's appearance startling. A classically beautiful face was framed by platinum blond hair, falling softly along one side of her face and turning under below her delicately curved jawline. The other side was brushed back, exposing a diamond earring.

Madelyn's black silk dress plunged daringly low. At one side of the neckline was pinned an enormous diamond broach. Her feet were elegantly encased in black pumps banded in gold.

Meeting people and making friends had always come easy for Norah, but Madelyn was another matter. Without another word, she retreated back into some shadowy place within herself.

Thornton took Norah's arm and steered her past the glass doors and into the game room, out of sight of the others.

"Have they seen Camille?" Norah asked.

"No," he replied curtly. "The next move is yours."

"What do you mean?"

"I told them that Lantz's child is here. Anything else is up to you."

Norah felt a wash of disappointment. Was Thornton so fearful of his family's reproach that he couldn't bring himself to tell them that Lantz had not married the mother of his child? Would the acceptance that Aunt Tess and Chris had offered her initially turn to the kind of coolness Madelyn had exhibited?

"Don't look so devastated, Norah," Thornton said. "Nobody's going to hurt you. We've had our share of skeletons in the family, and they haven't always stayed in the closet. The reason I said nothing is because I felt you would resent me even more if I mentioned you in some unfavorable way. Now," he went on with an impatient frown, "would you please allow my family to see their niece? The memorial service at church this afternoon was especially trying."

Norah's eyes dropped to the gritty sand between her toes, and she breathed deeply. Lest he see the moisture in her eyes, she turned her back on him.

He grasped her bare upper arms, and Norah stiffened. Rather than some reprimand, however, his words had the ring of an apology. "I thought you didn't want to go to the service, Norah. You also told me your reasons for avoiding your sister's funeral."

"It's all right," she said, suddenly aware of his fingers, now gently stroking away particles of sand from her arm. Something about that gentle action provoked a longing to be held in strong arms, like Camille, a helpless infant who needed acceptance and security.

But she was not a baby. Soon she would either have to lie to Eloise, Aunt Tess, and Chris . . . or tell the truth and chance Thornton Winter's rejection.

Suddenly, she remembered Madelyn. Why had she excluded her from that line-up of accepting people? What was she to Thornton Winter anyway? "I'd better dress for dinner," she murmured, moving out of his reach and heading for the bedroom.

Thornton rubbed his thumb across the tips of his fingers, feeling the sand from Norah's arm. His touch had been an involuntary effort to reach out to her. But he had not succeeded.

Strange that she seemed to have so little difficulty in relating to others. She had shown none of that belligerence with Aunt Tess and Chris, for example. She'd appeared to be a sensitive young woman, responding warmly to their overtures of friendship. Aunt Tess had obviously liked her on sight, and his aunt was a very discriminating woman.

He'd carefully watched Chris' reaction, too. His brother had been sincere in his compliments, which Norah had graciously accepted.

But Thornton? In spite of the fact that she needed his help, she seemed to fear him. She was undoubtedly the most stubborn, ill-tempered girl he'd ever known. Yet she was no girl! She was a woman who had attracted the attention of a mature man, a famous film star accustomed to being idolized by beautiful women. She'd captured Lantz's heart, at least long enough to conceive a child by him.

If she could so enthrall a man like Lantz Winter, how would a boy like Chris stand a chance? Thornton flexed his jaw, determined to put a stop to it before it started.

For her introduction to the family, Eloise had dressed Camille in one of her prettiest blue dresses with frills at the shoulders. Ruffled panties covered her diaper. Norah's heart swelled with love as she looked at her beautiful niece, who could beguile the strongest man and hold his heart in the palm of one tiny hand.

"I hope you don't mind," Eloise apologized when Norah sailed through the door.

"Oh, you're a lifesaver, Eloise," Norah breathed gratefully. "I had no idea they would come this early."

"They usually call from the dock," Eloise explained, "but I didn't know where you were on the beach, and you couldn't have gotten here before they arrived anyway."

"We'll just have to make the best of it." Norah sighed help-lessly. "Just let me wash this sand off my arms."

She returned from the bathroom, found a shirt, and slipped it on over her swimsuit, then held out her arms for Camille. "Where did you get that?" Norah asked, seeing the little blue bow tied around one of the golden-red curls.

"From a pair of her panties," Eloise confessed.

Norah laughed. "I won't tell." She buried her face in the baby's dimpled neck, inhaling the clean sweet smell. "I love you, my sweet." And cuddling her close as she walked back into the game room, Norah renewed her promise, "You're my baby, and I'll do everything in my power to keep you with me."

Thornton stood at the glass doors. He slid the door open for Norah, his eyes dancing with tenderness as he gazed at the beautiful baby. "May I?" he asked, and she laid Camille in the crook of his arm.

Beaming like a proud father, Thornton walked over to Chris, standing against one of the cedar posts. At his brother's approach, Chris turned. A surprised gleam leapt into his eyes. Reaching out, he touched the baby's soft pink arm, and she gurgled in response.

"Hey, we communicate on the same level," he said, elated. "Welcome to the family, little one."

His glance at Norah held a barrage of questions that went unasked. She sensed his discomfort and understood it instinctively. She had witnessed it many times while working at the clinic—the age-old question of why death strikes prematurely, robbing us of loved ones. She could see that Chris was trying to deal with his loss like a man. She longed to help him.

Norah followed Thornton as he carried the child over to Aunt Tess. "Lantz's baby," she breathed, her eyes misting. "Oh, look at those big blue eyes. And that gorgeous red hair. Oh, Norah dear, she is beautiful. You must be so proud."

An uneasy silence settled over the group. Thornton was right. This family wouldn't ask embarrassing questions, but she had to tell them something. For support, Norah grasped the back of the wooden chair in front of her. She knew she couldn't accept their friendship—Aunt Tess' and Chris'—with this barrier between them, this pretense that she was Camille's mother. Strangely, she also found herself wanting Thornton to know the truth, whatever its consequences. It would have to come out soon. Best they hear it from her.

"Norah, are you all right?" Aunt Tess asked with concern in her voice.

Norah nodded and cleared her throat. "I want you all to know," she began, glancing in Chris' direction, then scanning the faces of the others. Her lips felt dry, and she licked them. "I want you to know that Hillary Caine was really Hillary Browne. She is . . . was . . . my sister."

"Oh, my dear, I'm so sorry," Aunt Tess sympathized.

Chris pulled a chair out from the table, and Norah lowered herself into it. Then he sat down nearby. Aunt Tess extended her hand and Norah placed her own in it, finding strength in the comforting warmth.

Her courage left her, however, when Thornton walked around and stood behind Aunt Tess. Madelyn sat like a still-life painting in the background, with Eloise hovering near, ready to take the baby back into the house.

Norah darted a glance at Thornton, but his steady gaze was threatening rather than reassuring. *You have the right to remain silent,* his stiff stance seemed to be conveying. *Anything you say will be held against you.*

She swallowed hard, still staring into his face. "I am not Camille's mother," she began with trepidation and watched him flinch as if he'd been struck. Why did she feel like a murderer who had just confessed? She was guilty of nothing except love for an orphaned child. "But in my heart I *am* her mother," she insisted with conviction.

Thornton's expression didn't alter a whit. He simply looked down at Camille, who was fussing a little, and pursed his lips to make a soft clucking sound that quieted her.

"Camille belonged to Lantz and Hillary," Norah continued, looking to Aunt Tess for the courage to go on. "They were not married, but they loved each other very much." She glanced at Chris. Neither he nor Aunt Tess appeared shocked, only interested and sympathetic.

"I've been taking care of Camille since she was born, and I couldn't love her more if she were my own. I'm sure that . . ."

Aunt Tess interrupted with gentle praise. "You are very brave to take on such a heavy responsibility, Norah. It makes all the difference in the world, having that child here. Thank you," she choked, "for sharing her with us."

Share? How ironic, Norah thought. She had had no choice. Thornton Winter had forced her here against her will. And now she had no idea what he might do. She feared his power to take legal action. Even if his family sided with her, he had made it quite clear that this was his home and he would make the final decisions.

Without a glance in her direction, he moved toward Madelyn, carrying the baby in his arms.

"Oh, Thorn! Thorn!" Madelyn wailed and wrenched aside the glass door to run into the house.

Norah was instantly at Thornton's side and took the baby from him as he ran to catch up with Madelyn. His arms enfolded her, and she cried against his chest, then lifted a beautifully chiseled profile toward him, her ice-blue eyes brimming with tears.

At that moment, he turned his head and caught Norah's eye. He shrugged his shoulders eloquently, asking for patience in a glance. Then he led Madelyn, still clinging, down the hallway toward the front of the house.

"Could I hold the baby?" Aunt Tess asked gently, coming up behind Norah, as if the disturbing scene had not taken place.

"This is her wakeful time," Norah explained, "when she's most likely to be fussy."

"If you'll trust us, maybe Chris and I can handle her. And Eloise is a grandmother many times over, of course. You go right ahead and get dressed if you like."

With a smile of gratitude, Norah relinquished the baby to Aunt Tess and went quickly into the house. When she reached her bedroom door, the sound of soft sobbing and a deep masculine voice attempting to console reached her ears. Apparently Madelyn and Thornton were in the living room. She shook off the multitude of questions crowding her mind and went inside, closing her door behind her.

❧

Thornton was thoroughly confused. Even with Madelyn weeping pitifully in his arms, he could not forget the shocking scene he had just witnessed. What kind of mother would deny her own child? And if Norah were really Camille's aunt, she had lied to him! Who, and what, was the real Norah Browne? And how could Lantz have thought they had anything in common? But there was a more immediate problem confronting him.

"Oh, Thorn, how am I ever going to get through this?" Madelyn sobbed.

He continued to hold her close, patting her shoulder. "Time heals all wounds," he said rather distantly, grasping for anything that might sound comforting in this confusing time.

She lifted her lovely face. "All?" she whispered, seeing his scar, and a fresh torrent of tears erupted.

That wound was healing well. Another operation—some cosmetic surgery around his eye—and he might not appear so grotesque. But that was not the wound he felt so sharply. It was the inner hurts that still had not completely healed.

His arms tightened around Madelyn, but he glanced in the direction of Norah's bedroom. A lot in common, indeed!

ತ

Over an hour later, Norah sincerely hoped she was ready to present herself properly. After washing, drying, and brushing her coppery hair until it shone with sun-kissed highlights, she slipped into a dress she had always admired on Hillary and eyed herself critically.

Having applied makeup expertly in a manner she had learned from her mother, she knew she had maximized her best features. Her skin had deepened to a bronzed glow during the afternoon on the beach. It had been so long since she had taken time with her appearance that she had forgotten just how much she resembled her sister. At one time, Hillary had even suggested that Norah become her understudy, but Norah had refused. She had never felt comfortable on stage.

Looking at herself now, she knew Hillary would be pleased with the effect. The gold lamé tank dress came to just above her shapely knees. A crushed leather and metallic cumberbund grazed her hips, riding below her waistline and producing an easy flowing motion as she walked.

Finalizing the recreation of Hillary, she stepped into metallic high heels, slipped a brassy gold bracelet on her left arm and completed the effect with drop earrings. Deciding against the matching jacket, she brushed her waist-length hair around her shoulders and applied a bronzed gloss to her lips. Avoiding looking into her huge green eyes that belied this attempt at confidence, she sprayed perfume on her pulses, already beating erratically.

Taking a deep steadying breath, she told herself that Hillary wouldn't have been nervous. She would have swung out onto the deck and instantly become the center of attention, causing fragile beauties like Madelyn to fade into the woodwork.

But she was not Hillary. She was Norah, and Norah had a terrible attack of stage fright. She must face Thornton Winter as Camille's aunt. Suppose he said, "We can handle things from now on, Miss Browne. You should go on about your life, without the encumbrance of a baby."

Norah closed the bedroom door behind her and stood for a moment, leaning back against it, her eyes closed.

"Just when I decided your hair was permanently knotted on your head, you prove me wrong," said an all-too-familiar voice.

Norah's eyes flew open. Thornton rose from a chair in the game room. He'd been waiting for her! The inevitable confrontation would be now. His advance reminded her of a giant wave beginning far out in the ocean, coming closer, gaining height and strength. The sand was being pulled out from under her feet, and the undertow was threatening to drag her out into deep water.

She tried to back up, but there was no place to go. She did not want to fight him. "Please," she said, desperately wishing she could make her escape. "I need to see about Camille."

"The baby is perfectly content," he assured her, blocking her way.

Norah tried to step around him, but he reached out with one

big hand and encircled her arm, hauling her back. "I find you confusing, Norah Browne," he admitted. "In Florida, you were a high-spirited, indignant mother. Then, to impress my aunt and brother, you become a devoted, self-sacrificing young woman who is willing to give up her own freedom to care for her sister's child. Now, I find a glamorous Hollywood type trying to impress . . . whom, Miss Browne? Who are you, really? And what are you after?"

So he hadn't believed her when she told him she was Camille's aunt! She needn't have worried about his reaction to a lie. He didn't know the truth when he heard it. "What could I possibly be after?"

He shrugged. "Maybe the Lantz Winter estate," he said, and added mockingly, "a fortune for little Camille, of course."

Norah jerked her arm away, feeling the bedroom door against her back. "I'm not even aware there is a Winter fortune," she retorted.

"No?" he questioned. "I'd think Lantz would have told you."

"I don't know what Lantz might have told Hillary," she returned. "But he and I did not discuss such personal matters."

For a moment he almost believed her. Hillary would have been more Lantz's type—a public figure rather than a stay-at-home mother. "If you are really 'Aunt Norah,' you're every bit as convincing an actress as your sister. That mother-love act had me fooled." The smile on his lips was not pleasant.

"No, Mr. Winter," Norah contradicted. "It is you who have jumped to conclusions. You made the accusation. I simply didn't refute it."

A deadly quiet invaded the hallway. "All right," he conceded finally. "Just between you and me, who are you? Camille's aunt? Her mom?"

Norah lifted her chin. "Whomever she needs me to be," she said, her green eyes flashing.

"I'll tell you one thing," he said bluntly, "you may be a psychologist, but you need one."

"I am not yet a psychologist," she stated. "But I have been and will continue to be a mother to Camille. And I might add," she continued adamantly, "a father. I've been the only parent she's had for most of her young life."

That remark touched a sensitive chord, painfully reminding Thornton of his brother's lack of responsibility. "Just produce the birth certificate," he said wearily. "Perhaps there, I will find the truth."

"No," Norah countered, "if there is any proof to be provided, Mr. Winter, it will be you who supplies it. Prove that Lantz is Camille's father."

"Everything points to that fact." He quickly named the evidence. "The house in Florida. The photos of you, your sister, Lantz, and Camille. The pictures in his wallet. The confessions of a dying man. Proof enough," he affirmed. "You and I both know it."

"Exactly," she replied. She would not go so far as to deny Lantz's paternity. "But you can't prove it."

"Blood tests," he offered.

She shook her head. "Inconclusive. That would only prove that Lantz *could* be the father." A great surge of confidence bolstered Norah's claim, and her green eyes narrowed with challenge. "So you see, Mr. Winter, I don't have to prove I'm Camille's mother or her aunt. It is you who must prove that you are her *uncle*."

"If it comes to that, I believe I could scrape up enough evidence," he assured her.

"You make one wrong move, Mr. Winter," she threatened, "and this story will make the headlines of every newspaper across the country. Is that what you want for your niece?"

"Ah ha!" he said. "You wouldn't do very well in a court of law. You just admitted that Camille is my niece." His eyes held a triumphant expression. Then he added in a disarmingly gentle tone, "Maybe I could appreciate a devoted aunt, concerned about the welfare of her niece."

Was that possible? she wondered. Something warned her not to let down her guard. "Well, Mr. Winter, I can wonder if you are really a doting uncle or if you just prefer to keep a bevy of females around to persecute."

At that, Thornton threw back his head and laughed, then leaned forward to capture a tendril of hair between his thumb and forefinger. "With all this skepticism, Norah, I'd say you and I are on pretty equal footing, wouldn't you agree?"

She recognized the hint of amusement in his voice and saw a strange glimmer in his eyes. "No, Mr. Winter, I wouldn't say we're equal. Not financially anyway. But Camille is not into bank accounts. Nor are we equal when it comes to changing diapers, late-night feedings, or any other phase of child care."

Norah resented the condescending look on his face, as if her words were inconsequential. Perhaps they were. He could hire Eloise or others like her to do those things. She dropped her eyes to his suit coat, then lifted her face to his. "And who would play the mother role when you must leave the baby to meet . . . Madelyns . . . at the airport? Incidentally, you have a blond hair on your coat."

He looked down, picked it off, and let it float to the floor. "Be careful of that temper, Norah." He drew in a breath, looked around, then turned back and leaned closer as if sharing a secret. "You'd better be warned. Madelyn is not always as docile as she might appear."

"Really!" Norah declared in exasperation. "Are you trying to frighten me? You are very quick to make accusations about people. That is not a commendable characteristic."

His penetrating gaze left doubt as to whether he were serious. She suspected that he often deliberately provoked her.

Then her eyes found the reddened scar, and she made a wild, impetuous guess. "Did . . . did *she* do that?"

He nodded, then his dark lashes veiled his eyes and she couldn't begin to read his expression.

"What . . . what did you do to her, to cause it?" He gave a short laugh, and Norah explained, "I don't know when you're telling me the truth."

"Touché. We're equal on that score, Norah Browne, because there's a great deal I don't know about you." His eyes narrowed. "But I intend to find out."

"Is that some kind of warning?" she asked, bristling.

The wry smile left his lips and his dark eyes scanned her face. "Let's just say it's more of a promise."

His arm came up and his fingers lifted her chin. With torturous deliberation, he lowered his head and his sensitive mouth came closer. At his temples, the silver glints in his dark hair matched the glimmer in his mesmerizing eyes. For something to hold onto, Norah grasped the doorknob, aware of its coolness in her warm palm.

He galloped closer on the powerful, black stallion, his cape flying out behind him. She felt the vibration of thundering hoofbeats, heard the pounding in her ears. With a rush of force, he swept her up in his arms and bore her away. But he lost that fierceness as he gazed tenderly into her eyes, his lips so close she could feel his breath on her cheek . . . .

"Norah," he said huskily, "I want that birth certificate, and I want it *now*."

"You want . . . what?" she asked weakly.

"Camille's birth certificate," he replied and with a whimper of outrage at her own foolish fantasies, she wrenched the doorknob and stumbled backwards into the room.

Thornton broke his own fall by catching hold of the doorfacing. Gaining his feet again, he waited while Norah went to one of the boxes that was yet unpacked, rummaged through a sheaf of papers, then held out an official-looking document.

He took it from her, wondering what he would find. If she were Camille's mother and was as adamantly opposed to being in his home as she pretended, then she had some scheme in mind, such as threatening a scandal. If that turned out to be the case, he'd pay her off to leave the baby and the scandal behind her.

Looking down, he scanned the facts until he found what he was looking for. *Mother: Hillary Browne. Father: Unnamed.*

He straightened slowly. Norah was standing in the doorway, her back to him, her long flame-colored hair spread around her shoulders like a fire.

If circumstances were different, and if he were young like Chris or charming like Lantz, he might act upon the impulse he'd felt stir in him more than once. But he wasn't. She'd correctly diagnosed him when she assessed him as history, instead of a bird in flight, soaring freely over life's choppy waves.

He came up behind her. "Shall we join the others?" His words propelled her forward, toward the game room. She walked ahead, not looking back until he spoke again. "You and I, 'Aunt Norah,' must soon come to some kind of understanding."

With a toss of her head, she retorted, "I should think that by now you would understand."

Thornton understood more than she knew. He knew how frightened Norah Browne was of losing control of that baby. She had every right to be frightened. Everything considered, the possibility was strong that he would have to ask her to leave his home—without Camille.

six

Norah walked out onto the deck. An empty bottle sat on a table, while the contented baby sleepily surveyed her surroundings, her gaze coming to rest on Chris Winter's face as he looked down at her, making soft clicking sounds with his tongue. He had removed his suit coat and the towel slung across his shoulder was a clue that Eloise had instructed him in the art of burping babies. At Aunt Tess' tender expression, Norah realized anew the therapeutic value of Camille's presence in this family.

Chris looked up and gave a low whistle as Norah approached.

"Time for this little girl to be in bed," she said with a smile of acknowledgment.

He rose, still cradling the child awkwardly and walked with Norah toward the house. Glancing back and seeing Thornton's somber expression, the smile left her face. With a swift movement, her long hair swung around her shoulders and she hurried inside.

Thornton was staring at the empty doorway when he heard Aunt Tess' voice. "It's so good to have young people in the house again, isn't it, dear?"

He turned toward her and spoke thoughtfully. "She didn't want to come, Aunt Tess."

"Oh, Thornton," Aunt Tess said, rising from her chair and joining him. "You don't think she'll leave and take that baby, do you?"

He drew her close and enfolded her in a desperate hug. "No, Aunt Tess," he said, speaking over her head. "You know how I feel about family. Camille is my brother's child. The baby

73

stays with us."

Aunt Tess stepped back and looked up into his face. "Then Norah has decided to stay?" she asked expectantly.

"That remains to be seen," he said distantly. Aunt Tess decided not to probe and patted his arm. "Eloise said supper is ready when we are. Perhaps we shouldn't keep her waiting, dear."

Thornton smiled down at her. With his arm around her shoulders, they headed for the house. On the way he took time to be grateful for his aunt. She had always had a calming effect on him.

He could use some of that right about now, he decided. He was still puzzled about Norah's attitude toward him. How easily she and Chris had communicated, from the very first words exchanged. Chris had a way about him that reminded Thornton of Lantz. He tried not to be too envious as he stepped into the game room and heard the ripple of good-natured laughter from the young couple.

❧

Madelyn, at Thornton's right, was the last to join them at the dinner table. Norah, seated across from her, was not surprised when Thornton said, "Let us pray." After all, this was the Bible Belt she'd heard so much about, and the proper Thornton Winter would certainly adhere to tradition.

Norah closed her eyes and listened carefully. His prayer was brief. He invoked God's blessing on the food, asked for strength in these difficult days, and expressed gratitude for the blessings recently brought into their lives.

At the close, Chris' and Aunt Tess' soft "Amens" could be heard before the older woman spoke up, "That child is such a wonderful blessing, Norah."

Norah could honestly reply, "Yes, I've thanked God for her every day of her life, even prayed for her before she was born." She darted a meaningful glance at Thornton as if to let him know she had made a head start on prayer in Camille's behalf. His eyes met hers in a contemplative stare before turning his attention to his iced tea, squeezing some lemon into the glass and stirring. *As if he needed that!* she thought.

Aunt Tess patted her arm and smiled. While she and Chris unfolded their napkins, Madelyn sat motionless, gazing down into her plate. Responding woodenly to Thornton's whispered suggestion, she picked up her napkin and laid it in her lap.

Madelyn's bizarre behavior disturbed Norah. But more disturbing was Thornton Winter's earlier statement, "We must come to an understanding, Norah." The implied threat rolled around in her mind, taunting her.

Her troubled thoughts were interrupted by Eloise's appearance in the dining room, bearing a tray containing bowls of creamy broccoli soup which she set before them.

"Delicious," Norah said after the first taste.

Aunt Tess waited until Eloise left the room before saying under her breath, "You haven't met Hilda yet."

"I've heard about her," Norah acknowledged. "But if the food gets any better, I'll end up looking like a pumpkin."

There was a spattering of light laughter. Everyone joined in except Madelyn. Then Chris said, "Speaking of looks, Norah, I'm sure you've been told that you look enough like your sister to be her twin. I've seen all her films. Was she as nice as you?"

Norah shrugged off the compliment. "I know she loved your brother very much." *Had Madelyn loved him, too?* Norah wondered, noticing that the young woman had not taken a bite of her soup. Thornton glanced at Madelyn, then at Norah, a definite frown on his face, as if trying to convey a message.

Norah took her cue from Thornton. "I'd love to discuss Hillary with you sometime, Chris. I brought pictures with me."

Soon, Eloise was back with the main course—Veal Cordon

Bleu with mashed potatoes and rich brown gravy, tiny peas with pearl onions, and tomato aspic.

"Are you an actress too, Norah?" Aunt Tess asked.

"My dad says it has to be in your blood," Norah replied, adding, "so I suppose I missed those genes. Growing up, I was active in Children's Theater. Later, my big role was a lady's maid in 'Henry VIII,' which my father has played in numerous community theaters for as long as I can remember. Then, there were a few bit parts in movies. But acting was never an obsession with me like it was for Hillary and Lantz."

"That sounds fascinating, Norah," Aunt Tess said, to which Chris added, "I think it was in Lantz's blood."

A low moan came from Madelyn, followed by a silence that made Norah question whether she should be speaking so freely about a man who had been buried only yesterday.

"I do want to hear more about your sister, Norah . . . later," Aunt Tess said, with a significant glance toward Madelyn. "Suppose you tell us something more about yourself, dear."

A disturbing thought crossed Norah's mind. She was partaking of the Winter hospitality, as if this were a perfectly natural thing to do, when in fact Thornton Winter was close to being in control of not only Camille's fate, but her own. For an instant, she felt as empty as Madelyn appeared, and for the first time, Norah could empathize with her. Is that what happened to women who came under the Winter spell? But Aunt Tess was waiting, her silvery hair cocked to one side.

Remembering her plans and goals before encountering Thornton Winter, Norah launched into a recital of her studies in psychology, as she had to Thornton that night he had appeared out of the thunderstorm. "I plan someday to earn my Master's Degree in Psychology. I'd like to work with toddlers and adolescents."

"Such a worthy goal, Norah," Aunt Tess commended her. "Was there a particular reason why you chose that field?"

"Several. But the main reason was that, while I reject a career in acting for myself, I believe the use of drama can provide a healthy release of frustrations for children. Role playing, under the supervision of a trained psychologist, can be therapeutic in treating children with emotional disorders."

"Then that principle might apply to adults, too?" Thornton asked.

"So the studies indicate," she replied, noting his genuine interest. "It doesn't mean that all actors have psychological problems, of course, but studies have shown that such problems can sometimes be understood and treated through role playing."

"You may have hit upon something that helps me understand Lantz better. Maybe he needed that escape from some of life's hard realities," he observed, thinking of their parents' unexpected deaths.

Aunt Tess nodded. "Well, Norah, will you be going back to graduate school in the fall?"

Norah hesitated. From the corner of her eye, she could see Thornton's brooding dark eyes watching her over the rim of his glass. The best thing at the moment was to reply as if she still had control over her life. "If I stay in this area, I will need to find at least a part-time job and save some money before returning to school. There will be rent to pay, as well as other expenses, and I have to consider the amount of time I will need to spend with Camille."

Aunt Tess turned to regard her more closely. "I don't mean to pry, Norah, but," she glanced at Thornton, "what do you mean by 'rent to pay'?"

Thornton's curt rejoinder was immediately forthcoming. "Norah is being a bit dramatic, Aunt Tess. She and Camille are a part of the family now. Rent, of course, is out of the question." He gave Norah a scathing look.

Her red hair, gleaming in the light of the chandelier, swung about her shoulders as she quickly turned her face toward his. "As I've said before, Mr. Winter, you may contribute whatever you like toward Camille's support. I, however, intend to take care of myself and provide for the bulk of Camille's needs. I am not a babysitter, and until I can afford a place of our own, I expect to pay rent."

"Now, Thornton," Aunt Tess said uneasily, "if this is a problem, you know I have plenty of room in my house."

Thornton's scar turned a deep purple and Norah knew she had managed to infuriate him once more. Hoping to change the subject, she turned to Chris, who was attempting to suppress the grin tugging at his lips. "How about you, Chris? Are you in school?"

The conversation shifted to Chris' studies. He had two more years at the Citadel, where he was majoring in civil engineering.

"All Winter men have been Citadel graduates since its inception," Aunt Tess told her and continued with a brief overview of the family. Some had taken their places in civilian life, others in the military, but each was involved in some aspect of building and design, with the exception of Lantz.

Apparently, the Winter women and those who married Winter men had not been dominated by the males, as Norah would have assumed. Many were pioneers in their fields. Thornton's mother, for example, had played an active part in her husband's construction business, which included residences and deep-sea fishing vessels. And Aunt Tess, before her retirement last year, had taught English and Literature at the College of Charleston.

At that moment Eloise came in to remove their plates and serve dessert. The cherry cheese pie consisted of a melt-in-the-mouth, creamy filling sprinkled with pecans. Madelyn picked at hers, as she had throughout the entire meal.

"I would like to give Camille a homecoming present,"

Thornton announced over coffee. "What would you suggest, Norah?"

He would want it to be something meaningful, something practical. Lantz and Hillary had filled her closet with baby clothes before her birth and had bought her enough toys and stuffed animals to stock a toy store.

Norah knew the perfect gift. "Swimming lessons."

He seemed surprised. "Isn't she a bit young for that?"

"She's three months older than she ought to be. Immediately after birth is the best time to begin, Mr. Winter," Norah said. "Babies are accustomed to a watery existence before birth, so water is a natural element for them. Swimming lessons have saved the lives of many toddlers. And since you have a pool . . . and live near the ocean, it's doubly important."

Aunt Tess nodded approvingly, and Norah turned to Thornton for his opinion. He appeared quite thoughtful. "It was something Lantz wanted for Camille," Norah insisted. "I know he and Hillary talked about it even before she was born."

"Then perhaps we should consider it." Thornton wiped his lips on his napkin, indicating that the subject was closed for now.

Madelyn was fidgeting in her seat. "Excuse me," she said suddenly, pushing back her chair and hurrying from the room.

"Aunt Tess," Thornton began, "would you see about Madelyn? I'd like to talk with Norah . . . alone."

Thornton led her through the sliding glass doors to a secluded area of the deck, where they sat down in the padded redwood chairs. Glancing toward the sky, Norah saw faint pink streaks now quickly fading to gray. Feeling a chill in the air, she shivered.

"Cold?" Thornton wanted to know.

"Just cool. But I love it. Everything about the ocean is so invigorating to me." She breathed deeply of the tangy air.

"It certainly seems to agree with you," he said, eyeing her appreciatively. "You've improved considerably over that little girl in blue jeans with a braid on top of her head."

"Well, I'm a little more rested," she said, grateful for the cover of twilight. "I must admit I've enjoyed having a little time to myself for the first time since Camille was born."

"It's not so bad, is it?" he asked. "Being here?"

"As I told my parents when I called them Saturday," Norah returned, watching his lips form a taut line, "I'm grateful that Camille has this opportunity to *visit* her relatives."

"Visit?" The quirk of his eyebrow said it all.

Uncomfortable, she rose and walked over to the edge of the pool. Someone had turned on the underwater lights, and the surface shimmered in jeweled tones of blue and green.

Thornton joined her. "Camille's lessons should be given here if they start right away," he said. "If you want to take her to class, then it will be best to wait until after we move into town."

Norah chose not to take issue with that declaration, but gazed up at the sky, where a slice of moon had made its appearance in the darkening sky. "I'm not sure of the wisdom of your trying to make us such an integral part of your family."

Determination sounded in his reply. "I intend to do as Lantz asked and assure that his child is properly cared for. Don't you understand, Norah? Camille is all I have left of . . ."

He averted his eyes, but not before she saw his pain. He walked past her to the end of the deck, where he stood in the shadows, his body and shoulders taut. It was the first indication she had witnessed of how deeply Thornton Winter was feeling the death of his brother. She sensed that he was not a man who expressed his emotions easily.

Momentarily ignoring their differences, she walked up to him and touched his sleeve. "Mr. Winter," she said softly.

"Mr. Winter," he mimicked to cover his raw grief. "Even

Henry, a good thirty years older than I, is called by his first name. Is it because you respect me so much or . . . that you're more comfortable with the formality?"

"Yes, I . . . suppose that's it."

"And you're uncomfortable with *me*," he accused. "That's why you don't want to live here. That's why you're talking about renting a place, isn't it?"

"I only meant that I expect to be responsible for the two of us."

"I know what you said. But would you object if I offered you and Camille the beach house? For just the two of you?"

Norah did not glance away in time to hide the sudden elation that sparked her eyes.

"Or," he continued, "would you object if Aunt Tess asked you to live with her? Or even Chris? No," he answered for her, "it's *me* you object to."

Norah stared into the darkness. Thornton Winter was right. "Yes," she admitted. "It is you."

She turned her back on him and reached out to touch a leafy shrub.

He stepped up beside her. "What are you afraid of, Norah?"

"As you said earlier," she replied uneasily, "some things cannot be expressed simply."

"Try," he urged.

Norah drew in a breath of the cool night air. What was she afraid of? The reasons were fast becoming as numerous as the brilliant stars, shimmering in the deep blue sky. "I suppose I'm afraid of your controlling our lives. You're a very insistent man, Mr. Winter," she continued with a glance at him. "My wishes seem to make no difference to you."

"I realize I tend to be overbearing sometimes," he admitted. "But I doubt that you'd let me get away with that very often." Norah smiled faintly, responding to the surprising affability of this man who had before seemed so obstinate and unyielding.

"Or is it more personal, Norah? I know you are wary of me. I . . . frighten you. Are you afraid I will frighten Camille as she grows older? Is it my . . . face?"

The breath caught in her throat, painfully choking off the air. She could not speak for a moment. Finally she looked him directly in the eye. "Your looks," she said in a whisper, "mean nothing to a child. Or to me. Actually, it is your face that has kept me from being terribly frightened of you."

He turned the scarred side from her. "I'm not seeking sympathy or some false sense of acceptance from you, Norah," he said with difficulty.

"I know," she said. "And I'm so sorry if I've given the impression that it bothers me. I know I've stared. That's only natural. Curiosity is one of my weaknesses, perhaps. Look at me, please."

He turned reluctantly.

Her voice was very gentle. "It is your face that has made me aware that you are a vulnerable, suffering human being like the rest of us, and . . . capable of being hurt."

Thornton reached for her hand and held it between his palms. "I don't want you to be frightened of me, Norah. For any reason."

"I was never frightened for myself . . . Thornton." His name fell easily from her lips.

Soft moonlight danced in his eyes, subduing the harsh contours of his handsome face. His lips formed a wide smile and she felt a breathlessness that was almost dizzying.

"I want to do the right thing," Norah heard herself saying, and the sound of her own voice surprised her. Of course, she wanted to do the right thing. But how had she come to the point of giving in to Thornton Winter's wishes? Startled by her own thoughts, she lifted her eyes to his and found them to be dark and foreboding again.

"That's not always easy to know," he said. A shudder ran

through her. Thornton looked toward the house, at the bird-in-flight design. He hated what he had to do, what he had to say. "Norah, you are to be commended for what you've done in caring for Camille during the past three months. This terrible tragedy has brought out your remarkable characteristics. But, no one would blame you for just being an aunt, like Aunt Tess. She's an invaluable member of our family, you know."

Thornton saw fear and frustration replacing her beginning acceptance. But the only decent thing to do was to try and make her understand. "You're not obligated to take on this responsibility. You're young, beautiful, single, and you deserve the freedom that goes with it."

Of all the options that might be open, Norah was beginning to believe that the security offered by Thornton Winter was best for Camille. *But not without me!* her heart screamed. *Oh, please, not without me!*

He saw the brave lift of her determined chin. "No one would blame you," he said, and she felt the twist of a knife with each word. "Rearing a child takes personal sacrifice."

"I know all that," she said helplessly.

"No, you don't," he retorted. "You've had three months of caring for a beautiful, perfect baby. And when it changed suddenly, drastically, irreversibly, you made an admirable decision based on loyalty to your sister, love for your niece, and personal loss."

"And what about you?" she asked desperately.

"I've faced this situation before, remember? I know what I'm getting into. I became Chris' legal guardian when he was eleven and Lantz was sixteen. But you need to think seriously before the child becomes too attached to you. I don't want you deciding later on that your personal freedom has been hampered, or that you're really not up to this. Once you take on that responsibility, Norah, nothing is ever the same."

He knew no way to say these things tactfully. "I want you to think about the situation while I'm away for a few days. You can give me your answer when I return."

She'd almost believed that Thornton Winter was a Dracula, for this man's overwhelming power to shake her confidence was uncanny. But he was not the caped vampire. She knew now that she had no reason to fear him. But she would fight for Camille, if necessary.

She squared her shoulders. "How old are you, Mr. Winter?"

"Thirty-four."

"That's not exactly ancient," she observed. "You deserve a life of your own too." Her eyes blazed. "And one more thing— just what do you know about bringing up little girls?"

His dark eyes glittered and his tone was brittle. "I seem to be having more trouble with *big* girls than little ones."

Norah bristled. "Camille and I are a package deal. Do you really want two extra females under your roof for the next twenty years? It seems to be getting crowded around here."

That remark seemed to hit a sensitive spot, but before he could answer, dazzling light splashed onto the deck. His marred face took on a ghostly pallor as he faced the house. Inside, a figure in black paced restlessly.

"Is Madelyn really dangerous?" Norah asked, once more aware of the cooling breeze.

"Ah, Norah," he said, watching Madelyn, "isn't every attractive woman potentially dangerous?"

With this evasive maneuver, Norah's delight in finding an equal footing with Thornton Winter turned to doubt. What had happened to the warmth and tenderness she thought had passed between them? Had she imagined it? For now he seemed far removed, as if some shadow had settled upon him.

"Let's go inside," he said abruptly and without waiting for a reply, preceded her to the house.

Norah remained in the shadows, her eyes following the retreating figure of the man who could dispatch compliments and criticism with equal fervor. She watched him slide the door open and move inside where the woman was waiting for him. He bent his tall frame toward Madelyn, and his arm encircled her shoulders. Her blond head tilted upward and her body melted into his with an unmistakable intimacy before they moved out of sight.

Norah hugged her arms to herself. She wanted desperately to trust Thornton Winter. And she had. For one brief moment. Long enough for him to expertly manipulate the situation. She had all but admitted her acceptance of him, had called him by his first name, had tacitly accepted his hospitality without charge. But at what cost to her pride and independence? And how quickly Winter charm could turn to Winter chill!

seven

Norah let out a gasp of fright when the bang of the sliding glass doors broke her concentration. The gasp subsided to a sigh of relief when Chris walked out onto the deck and looked around.

Spotting Norah, he called out to her. "Thornton said it was getting chilly out here and asked me to bring you a sweater. I had Eloise get this for you." Strolling over to join her, Chris shrugged it around her shoulders. "You *are* cold. Want to go inside?"

"I'd rather stay out here for a while," she said with a sigh.

"Mind if I join you?"

"I'd like that, Chris," she replied, and they moved toward the house where they would be sheltered from the breeze.

"Be right back," he promised. "I'll get us something warm to drink."

Norah settled back against the cushions of the chair, forcing her thoughts to the days ahead, when she and Camille would be able to enjoy this lovely setting without the unsettling presence of Thornton Winter. Perhaps then she could rid herself of the foolish thoughts that had invaded her mind tonight—that Thornton was some devious monster about to steal Camille from her. And maybe she could even bring herself to believe that he was only trying to help Madelyn, a distraught woman whose emotions lay very near the surface. Though Norah could not be sure what Madelyn's relationship with Lantz had been, she could understand something of what she must be feeling. From Norah's experience with Roman, she knew that the loss of a friend could be as heartbreaking as the loss of a relative.

This is only a bad case of nerves, she told herself. Perfectly understandable. In a matter of mere days, she had lost her sister and a friend, had become a surrogate mother, had encountered the enigmatic Thornton Winter, and had exchanged her simple lifestyle for one utterly foreign to her.

My imagination is working overtime, she thought. *That's all it is.* And as if to prove it, a smiling Chris emerged from the house, bearing mugs of steaming hot chocolate topped with marshmallows.

"So tell me about Hillary," Chris said as they sipped the warm beverage. "What was she like in real life?"

While the question focused on her sister, Norah had the feeling he wanted to talk about his brother. Her assumption was correct, for soon he was asking questions about Lantz and his relationship with Hillary. Norah answered as honestly as she knew how. "Would you like to see those pictures now?"

When they went inside, Aunt Tess and Thornton were talking in the game room, and Madelyn was nowhere in sight. Aunt Tess hugged her. "I want you to know, Norah, that I am quite impressed with you, taking care of Camille the way you have. That shows a great deal of strength and depth of character. Now, we're here to help, dear, so feel free to call on me any time you need me."

"Thank you so much, Aunt Tess," Norah replied, feeling a warm rush of gratitude.

"Could I stay for a while?" asked Chris, coming up beside her.

Thornton hesitated. "If it's all right with Norah, Chris."

"Of course."

"Just don't forget there's a baby in the house," Thornton said, looking stern, "and keep down the noise."

"Oh, I'll take care of the baby, Mr. Winter," she said pseudo-sweetly, and lifted her accusing eyes to his. "And you have a good evening now."

Unaccountably irritated, Thornton Winter turned and stalked down the hallway. Why shouldn't he have a good evening? After all, he wasn't "ancient."

Norah brought out a picture album and sat down beside Chris on the couch. As they turned page after page, Chris began to open up, confiding in Norah the pain of losing Lantz so soon after the death of his parents. Norah cried with him, then found herself telling Chris about Roman, her young friend who had died of leukemia. "Roman was closer to God and a greater witness for Him as he was dying than most people when they are alive."

"I knew I could talk to you, Norah," Chris said, no longer trying to hide his tears.

"I'd like to be your friend, Chris." No matter how much Norah might resemble her sister, she wanted him to know the real person within.

When Chris looked up, his clear blue gaze was utterly transparent. "I hope you and Camille stick around, Norah," he said. "She makes me feel like Lantz is still with us."

She nodded and closed the book. It seemed everyone wanted her to stay . . . everyone, that is, except Thornton Winter.

Chris stretched and got to his feet. "I'd better be going. School starts tomorrow. But maybe I'll see you over the weekend."

"I hope so," Norah said sincerely. "Good night, Chris."

She heard him drive away, and the house grew strangely quiet. She opened the album once more and studied a photo of Lantz and Hillary taken only days before their deaths. "What would you want me to do?" she whispered to the beautiful images.

Suddenly, sensing a movement, she looked up, startled, as Thornton walked into the room. "What are *you* doing here?"

"I live here, remember?" he informed her and stepped nearer to view the pictures.

"Uh . . . I mean . . ." She peered around him. "Where's your friend?"

He scowled, reaching down to lift the book from her lap. "Aunt Tess is taking Madelyn home," he said shortly. "I decided I could leave from here in the morning." He sat on a stool, flipping through the pictures.

Norah slid onto the stool next to him, ready to offer explanations.

Thornton stared at a picture of Lantz and Norah, snapped by Hillary, and decided he would not mention Chris' youthful vulnerability. Once, during the evening, he had come down the stairs undetected and had overheard Chris' lament, Norah's warm consolation.

"Quite a few women found Lantz irresistible," Thornton said at last, breaking the awkward silence. "What about you?"

Norah shrugged. "There was never anything to resist. He was in love with my sister, not with me."

"And how did you feel about him?" he pressed.

She thought for a moment. "Lantz was a lot like Chris, I think, warm and open. A very decent man."

"But he . . . wasn't your type?"

She wasn't sure what he was getting at. "I liked Lantz very much. We shared a similar association with show business, but took opposite views of it." She shrugged once more. "He and I just didn't have much in common."

Thornton thumbed through the pages, remembering what Lantz had said. *You and Norah have a lot in common.* For the life of him, he still couldn't figure out what that could be. A dual personality? Stubborn pride? Perhaps instead of a compliment, Lantz had intended it as a warning!

❧

Thornton, in suit and tie, stood at the glass door, drinking his orange juice. His gaze was riveted on Norah and Camille at the edge of the patio where Henry was pulling weeds from a flower bed. In the wash of early-morning light, everything glistened with a luminescence that created an aura about the two bright heads. Finishing his juice, he set the glass on the nearest table and stepped outside.

Norah turned to greet him. Her hair, like a vibrant flame, swung softly against the free-flowing sundress of lemon yellow. In her arms, Camille looked adorable in a white knit sleeper, trimmed in lace.

"Good morning!" Thornton's mood was reminiscent of that morning in Florida, when he had seemed so energetic and ready for the day. Camille stared at him with eyes wide and clear as a bluebell. "And how are you this morning, little flower of my heart?" He kissed the back of her hand. "Say hello to Uncle Thorn."

They laughed together in delight as Camille gurgled happily in reply. Thornton touched the plump pink cheeks. "Picture perfect," he said, glancing up at Norah and leaving her to wonder whom he was addressing. "You slept well?"

"Probably not as well as you, after your late-night swim. I saw you pass my window, headed for the beach." That had been another glimpse of Thornton Winter, so different from his usual stiff, unyielding stance, a side of him that she'd discovered only last night was a defense against pity. The glimpse of him in his swimsuit, however, had rendered nothing surprising.

Not surprising—but disturbing. Disturbing, because she had been tempted to join him on that deserted beach beneath the silver moon, to manipulate a confrontation with Thornton Winter that would let him know how strongly she was drawn to him.

But, Norah reminded herself, she was not an actress like Hillary. She had never aspired to be Hillary's understudy, had never desired a secondary role, to stand in the wings, looking on wistfully, hoping, wishing. . . .

Besides, in this scenario there was already a leading lady—a serenely beautiful blonde whose soft blue eyes constantly sought the tender glance, the protective, caring arms of Thornton Winter.

"I didn't go down to the beach for a swim," he was saying, returning her to the present. "I needed to run."

He'd needed to think, too. After his run, he'd sat on the beach while the cool breeze dried the sweat that had curled his hair into damp ringlets and glistened on the dark hair of his body. He'd felt physically exhausted, but exhilarated, too.

Looking toward the night sky that blanketed the white-foamed waves, he had thought of the questions Norah had raised. In another year, Chris would be twenty-one, and Thornton could consider making a life for himself in a way he hadn't been able to for the past twelve years.

Had he been too hasty? At Lantz's deathbed, he'd had the noblest of intentions. Promising to care for Camille had seemed the right decision at the time. Now, aware of Norah's fierce opposition to his good intentions, he'd had some second thoughts about his promise.

Furthermore, he had to consider what was best for all of them. He had prayed about the matter and thought the answer was clear. If he could prevent it, he would not want Camille to be denied the kind of love Norah could give her. But the decent thing to do was to offer Norah a choice.

"I'll be at the office most of the day," he said abruptly, getting to his feet. "Then I have to fly to California and Florida regarding some legal matters pertaining to Lantz's estate."

"How long will you be away?"

"It's hard to say. Several days maybe. But I won't always be this busy. Soon I'll be able to spend more time with Camille."

Norah nodded, understanding. "She sleeps most of the time

right now anyway."

"Then you should take some time for yourself, Norah. You've had a very demanding schedule for three and a half months. You deserve a little time off to rest . . . and think!"

"I—I'll do that."

He glanced at her in alarm. She meant it, and the thought did not bring the satisfaction he would have expected. Suppose, when he returned, she said, "She's all yours, Mr. Winter?" He felt shaky, clear down to his black conservative shoes. Whatever her choice, Thornton's life would be irrevocably changed.

He leaned down and kissed Camille on the forehead. "Byebye, little one," he said gently, then searched Norah's eyes, feeling compelled to say, "Please don't try anything foolish."

The sudden defiant tilt of her chin and the ramrod-stiff spine indicated she had understood him. She still would not be permitted to leave the island with Camille. If she went, she'd go alone.

But this time, no explosive response was forthcoming. Was she beginning to trust him? Or was she resigning herself to leaving—without Camille?

Norah held the baby close and watched Thornton Winter disappear into the house. "You smell like musky aftershave," she murmured to the little girl.

The fragrance lingered. So did his words.

Nothing foolish, he'd said. Norah wasn't too sure which would be more foolish—leaving . . . or staying.

❧

On Tuesday, after making an appointment for Camille with a pediatrician and learning that the hospital in Charleston would forward literature on teaching infants to swim, Norah invited Aunt Tess for lunch.

As soon as Camille was settled for her nap, the two women took a dune buggy tour of the island, only ten miles long and five miles across at its widest point. The lazy afternoon, warmed by the sun, invited an exchange of confidences, and Norah found herself wondering aloud, "Isn't it amazing that Thornton could have built such a marvelous place on such a desolate stretch of land?"

"He's the best designer in the business, even if he is my nephew," Aunt Tess said proudly. "He designed the beach house before he finished college."

Aunt Tess parked the vehicle and got out. In a sleeveless dress and sandals, the light wind stirring her short gray hair, she looked younger than she had on Sunday. "My brother Thaddeus was Thornton's father," she said as they strolled along the beach, watching the sailboats bobbing on the water. "He was a designer and builder of ships, like his ancestors before him. But after everything passed down to Thornton, he sold the shipping business and concentrated on private homes."

Norah admitted a lack of knowledge in that area, but added, "It does seem extraordinary for one so young to have designed that beach house."

"Thaddeus was a perfectionist," Aunt Tess explained. "His stipulation for partnership was that Thornton design a house that he could approve."

"Apparently he succeeded."

"Well, Thaddeus declared that he himself would never have come up with such a design. But he admitted that he didn't have Thornton's kind of originality. Then he welcomed him into the business and told him to go ahead and build the house and furnish it—as his graduation present!"

"What a wonderful story, Aunt Tess."

"To that point, Norah," she said sadly. "Thaddeus never saw the place completed. Right after that, he and Caitlin were in a terrible boating accident and were killed instantly."

"That had to have been a terrible shock for all of you," Norah said softly.

"Particularly for the younger boys," Aunt Tess recalled. "My husband and I would have taken them, of course, but Carter wasn't well, and Thornton insisted on caring for his brothers himself and keeping them in the family home." At Norah's quick glance, Aunt Tess added, "Carter died of a heart attack four years ago."

Norah murmured her condolences, then she went on. "Do you think that was the right decision, Aunt Tess? Keeping the boys at home, I mean?"

"Well, Thornton was only twenty-four when he became their legal guardian," she admitted. "But as much as possible, he enforced the rules by which Thaddeus and Caitlin had raised him. He involved himself in his brothers' activities, managed the family business, took the boys to church every Sunday, and limited his social life drastically."

Aunt Tess gazed out over the sparkling water crested with whitecaps, like swirls of icing on a cake, before moving on down the beach. "Looking back," she continued reflectively, "I believe it was best. Carter and I were here to help when needed. But Thornton preserved a sense of family, particularly for himself and Chris. He is a brother, but he's also a father figure for Chris."

Watching the white-winged seagulls sailing so effortlessly over the sea—dipping, swooping, diving at some succulent morsel—Norah realized that Thornton's beach house was a symbol of the kind of freedom he himself had rarely known. The kind of freedom he was offering her. And by the time they returned to the house, Norah had a deeper understanding of Thornton Winter. However—and her chin went up at the thought—she did not intend to sit idly by and wait for him to deliver ultimatums and make all the decisions. She had some options of her own!

"Aunt Tess," she said, her green eyes alive with enthusiasm. "Tell me more about the College of Charleston."

On Wednesday morning, Norah drove the dune buggy to the ferry, where Aunt Tess met her. Beneath a clear blue sky, they rode through the small town of Mt. Pleasant, ablaze with delicate crimson, purple, and pink azalea blossoms. The intricate steel girders of the majestic Cooper River Bridge took them into Charleston and to the main campus of the College that Aunt Tess said included eighty-six buildings and extended over seven city blocks.

The campus was impressive. Mellow brick buildings nestled alongside wooden ones. Courtyards and old-fashioned lamp-posts gave an aura of the past, while renovated buildings offered the latest in technology.

Aunt Tess had called ahead to make an appointment, and the two women were welcomed into the dean's office, where Dr. Joshua Logan, the head of the Psychology Department, was waiting to talk with Norah and give her a tour of the campus. Dr. Logan, a big man with rust-colored hair and a thick curly beard, reminded Norah of lumberjacks she had seen in the movies.

While Aunt Tess stayed behind to talk with the dean, Dr. Logan led Norah into his office. She liked him right away. His deep, resonant voice and the spark of merriment in his dancing brown eyes gave her the impression that a class under him would never be boring.

He told her about the Psychology Department and of his own plans for the fall. He would be returning to the mountains of western North Carolina to take a position at the University of North Carolina. Though it would mean a cut in salary, he would be going home. "But enough about me. Let's see what we can do for you," he said. "And let's get the formalities out of the way. Call me Josh. I have an idea we're going to be good friends."

After discussing the possibility of Norah's attending classes in the fall, and the prospect of her finding a job or getting financial aid, Josh said, "How about some lunch? I can offer you a cafeteria line like none other."

Aunt Tess was in her element, seeing fellow teachers with whom she had worked so many years. Several of them had invited her to join them in the cafeteria, so she waved Norah away with a smile. Over lunch, Norah briefly related her situation and discovered a kindred spirit in Josh Logan. One of his reasons for moving back home was to investigate the unsolved murder of his sister. "At the end of the summer, I'll be giving up my part-time job as youth director at my church. Would that interest you?"

Norah glanced at him with growing appreciation. There was more to this man than met the eye. "I'm afraid it would require more time than I have to give," she said, and told him about Camille.

Josh was sympathetic. "That accident was the talk of the campus for a while. I've heard of your sister, of course, but with my classes and church activities, I don't see much TV or movies. By the way," he added, smiling broadly, "you need to get involved with people, Norah. And if you haven't found a church yet, check us out. We have a fine nursery. I'd be glad to meet you there and show you around."

Norah was touched. "If Mr. Winter hasn't returned from his trip by Sunday, I just might do that."

Josh looked up from his plate. "You're talking about Thornton. Winter, the builder?"

"That's the one."

Impressed, he raised his eyebrows. "I heard he was engaged to marry some woman he's known for a long time."

"Engaged?" Norah froze, completely unprepared for that revelation. How could she have been so naïve? Thornton had told her only that he didn't have a wife. But he hadn't mentioned a fiancée.

Of course. Madelyn. Madelyn was in his house. In his

arms. Obviously in his heart.

And Norah was . . . in his way. Was that his real reason for wanting her to leave? So he could get on with his life? She felt the blood drain from her face. "What do you know, Josh?" she asked. "It's of the utmost importance."

"Practically nothing, really. It was probably just a rumor anyway," he said, seeing the anguish on her face. "Hey, I've put my foot in it, and I'm sorry."

Norah lost her appetite, and Josh quickly finished his lunch and gave her the promised tour. But her mind was not on the interesting lecture or the charming lecturer, and when they got back to his office, he gave her his business card. "If you ever need a friend, Norah, call me."

"Thanks," she said weakly. "I may take you up on that."

"Good. Then I hope to see you Sunday morning."

❧

Norah's mom and dad called on Saturday, during an afternoon rainstorm, to say that Thornton Winter had stopped by to see them. Both Nancy and Frederick Browne were obviously fascinated with him, thought him to be a most generous man, and were pleased that he had claimed Norah and Camille as part of his family.

Norah was glad to hear from them, and it confirmed what she already knew—that they were not interested in bringing up another family. She couldn't blame them. After all, they'd be in their seventies before Camille finished high school. Yes, Thornton's visit had definitely put their minds at ease about Camille's welfare—and Norah's.

Obviously, he hadn't told them the whole story—that he had asked her to consider leaving his home—without Camille.

"You're a lucky girl," Nancy said, and her singsong tone led Norah to believe her mother suspected some kind of romantic involvement. "We just might pop down there soon, but we have another tour starting next week. I'll call and give you a phone number."

"Don't worry about us, Mom," Norah assured her. "We're fine. Just have fun."

"Take lots of pictures," Nancy said. "We do want to keep up with our granddaughter."

And that's what Norah was doing when Thornton returned Sunday afternoon.

eight

While Camille napped, Norah lounged on the deck in shorts and T-shirt, reading a book Josh had given her that morning at church. Though the book, *Undivided* by Trevor Steinborg, was a work of fiction, the story was incredibly true to life.

Hearing Camille's sleepy cry, Norah went to take her out of her crib and bring her outside, laying her on a quilt in the shade by the pool, then offering her cuddly animals to distract her. Quickly tiring of her toys, the baby became fascinated with the white clouds floating by in a sky as blue as her eyes.

Norah lay beside her, snapping picture after picture, until she heard the sliding glass doors open. She assumed it was Eloise. Couldn't be Henry, because he was asleep in a chaise lounge, his newspaper over his chest and his mouth hanging open like a flycatcher.

Not until he spoke did she realize it was Thornton. "Is this the way to greet a man when he returns to his castle after a week on the road?" he asked with mock gruffness. "Eloise is asleep in front of the TV. Henry is either snoring or pretending to be a frog. And Aunt Norah is lying on her back, taking pictures of the sky!"

Norah laughed, bringing the camera down from her eyes.

Thornton felt an overwhelming sense of well-being. The week had been difficult, but had brought closure to a part of his past. Then, driving here from the airport, he had realized that spring had arrived in all its intoxicating lushness. Flowers and gardens and fruit trees were in riotous bloom. The sun was dazzling, the sky brilliant, the air warm and fragrant.

After reaching the island, he'd felt a lightness in his spirit

that was new and refreshing. "Going home" had taken on a
broader significance. And now round blue eyes and oval green
ones stared up at him. For the moment, he actually felt like a
king.

Norah pulled herself into a sitting position, her long pony-
tail swinging over her shoulder. "Camille wanted me to take
pictures for her memory book," she said. Her voice was light,
like the breeze that stirred the air and cooled his cheek. "Look,
she thinks the clouds are a new toy."

Thornton knelt beside Camille and gently moved his finger
from one red-gold ringlet to another. "Hello, beautiful. How's
my little girl?"

In response, Camille began to blow bubbles and shake her
fists, until one landed in her mouth.

Norah snapped the picture. Thornton looked startled and
his scar turned purple. Suddenly she realized why. He was
thinking of his face. Were it not for Camille, she felt he'd
have grabbed the camera and flung it into the pool.

"Please don't take my picture again," he said stiffly, trying
to restrain his rage for Camille's sake.

"You should be ashamed of yourself, Thornton Winter,"
Norah scolded as gently as possible. "You're ten times better-
looking than most men with both sides of their face as smooth
as a snake's belly."

At that, he burst out laughing. "You call that a compliment?"

"No," she said. "It's a fact. You need to talk about it,
Thornton, and get it out of your system." He also needed to
rid himself of a few other things that contributed to his gloom,
Norah thought, having decided that Josh's comment about
Thornton's alleged engagement was nothing more than a
rumor. Or else it was a part of his past, and not a very happy
part, she judged.

Thornton wondered if she realized she had called him by

his first name. But he mustn't put too much stock in that, for he knew how quickly that acceptance could change to rejection. "I don't like to have my picture taken," he reiterated coolly.

"Well, that's too bad. I happen to be taking pictures for Camille's grandparents." Norah's voice grew soft. "The baby looks at you with eyes of love, you know."

He didn't reply right away, then changed the subject. "I met your parents."

"Yes, they called."

"They send their love."

Camille was staring up at him, her eyes growing heavy, and Norah sat down beside her and drew her legs up under her. "My parents think it's wonderful that Camille and I are here."

"I know," he said. "In fact, I learned quite a bit about you while I was there. For instance, I learned that you were greatly influenced by your grandparents."

Norah gazed up at the sky, looking for faces in the clouds. "I miss them so much," she said wistfully. "I always felt I had to act to gain my parent's approval. But with my grandparents . . . well . . . I could just be myself."

"Camille gives you the same feeling, doesn't she?" he asked. "That incredible feeling of being accepted and loved, just for who you are."

They smiled down at the sleeping baby between them.

Suddenly Henry snored loudly and woke himself up. Looking startled, he folded his paper abruptly and sat up on the edge of the chaise. He stared at Thornton and Norah as if they were strangers. "That baby should be in her bed," he proclaimed. "I'll send Eloise out." And he left without a backward glance.

Thornton shook his head and Norah chuckled. "Henry's teaching Camille all about plants," she said.

"He's the expert." He moved to a nearby chair when Eloise

came to collect the baby.

"This may surprise you, Thornton," Norah began after the housekeeper had disappeared through the glass doors, "but I've been thinking about the options you presented."

"And what have you decided?" He waited for her answer with a considerable amount of apprehension.

"I know about your becoming a parent at a young age, so I understand your reasons for saying what you did to me. The realization is dawning that parenting is more frightening than I had thought. It's really a willingness to give up your life, if necessary, for the benefit of another, isn't it? That's pretty overwhelming."

Thornton looked toward the house, unwilling to meet her green gaze. If she'd decided to be an aunt instead of a mother, he couldn't blame her. She was not obligated.

Her voice dropped. "It really will require more of me than I had realized."

Thornton remained quiet, his mind racing. Had he overdone it? Made her feel she was inadequate? She wasn't, of course. But this was her decision.

Norah took a deep breath and faced him squarely. "I've come to understand that I don't have exclusive rights to Camille." Her chin lifted in that brave little show of defiance. "But I'm more determined than ever to keep her with me. I've bonded with that child as if she were my own. I can't leave her. You can't ask me to. And I won't try to take her away as long as I feel this is best for her. Right now," she finished quietly, "I do."

"Norah!" he exclaimed, the force of her name expressing his gratitude and relief. She wasn't going to make things difficult for him, wasn't planning to initiate a court fight. But he knew that her decision hadn't been an easy one. When you'd lost someone dear to you, it was only natural to try to hold on to people—even things—very tightly. That was reflected in the position of her hands, now clasped together, her knuckles white.

"Norah," he repeated softly. "I love her, too, you know."

"I know." His love for Camille was evident in his voice when he spoke to her, in his eyes when he looked at her.

"Does this make you sad, Norah?" he asked gently.

"More scared than sad," she admitted. "But as long as I feel things are working in Camille's best interests, I'm not leaving . . . but that doesn't mean I won't make my share of the decisions about her welfare," she added quickly.

"I understand that." Norah would share, but she would not relinquish complete control. Nor would she let down the barriers that had been raised from the moment they had met. She was wary of entrusting Camille's future to him. She was taking a chance . . . on him. It was a major breakthrough. Thornton was elated.

"I appreciate what you said about sharing, Norah. And I don't want to take anything from either of you. I want to give."

He stood and filled his lungs with the fresh spring air. He had an overwhelming urge to lift her to her feet and hug her in gratitude, to assure her that he had no ulterior motives. He wanted the best . . . for all of them.

His eyes fell on the novel lying on the table, and he picked it up. *"Undivided.* You're reading this?"

"Yes. Josh Logan gave it to me," she said, and his head snapped around. "He said you might want to read it, too."

"Josh Logan? Who's he?"

"Oh, well you see," she began happily, "in making my decision, I also decided to be working on my life, too, not just sitting around waiting for you to make all the plans."

She had expected him to joke with her, but his countenance darkened, the scar making a vivid streak down his face. "Who is this Josh Logan?" he asked again.

"Josh? Oh, he's a psychology professor at the College of Charleston. Aunt Tess introduced us last week."

"So he gave you the book then?"

"No," she replied, finding this exchange bewildering. "He gave it to me this morning, at church."

"You went to church?"

"C-h-u-r-c-h," she spelled.

"Don't patronize me, Miss Browne," he warned. "Where did you go to church?"

"In Mt. Pleasant."

He looked like a thunderstorm about to erupt, the dark clouds gathering in his eyes. "Why?" he asked stiffly, his tone giving fair warning that the storm was about to break.

"Why?" she asked, forcing her voice not to betray her confusion. "Because I'm a Christian."

He shook his head. "I mean, why that particular church?"

"What's wrong with it?" she asked, beginning to grow irritated. "Did I stumble on to some kind of cult or something?" Then, "If you must know, I felt strengthened and inspired by the sermon, and the music was a medley of old hymns that I haven't sung in a long time."

He was shaking his head. "That's not the point. I'm sure there's nothing wrong with the church. It's just that I assumed that if we were going to cooperate, you would wait until we move to my house in Charleston and go to my church there. . . ."

"You mean the one you didn't invite me to for Lantz's memorial service?"

He drew back as if she had struck him. "I've already apologized for that. It was a mistake. At the time, I thought you were an unwed mother who wouldn't want to face the crowds."

"Nevertheless," she insisted, "I would like to have been asked. I was invited to the church in Mt. Pleasant." Her voice continued to rise. "That makes a difference, Mr. Winter. It's important to feel wanted. Besides, I wouldn't want to take Camille to some stuffy old historic church, as dull as dust. . . ."

"And are you in the habit of passing judgment before you've had a chance to see for yourself?" he demanded.

"No," she admitted. "It's an impression based on . . ." She hesitated, then grabbed the book he was still holding and brushed it off. "Anyway, I was impressed with the nursery facility, and that's an important part."

"I have no quarrel with the church itself," Thornton went on, striving for control. "It's just that this is the most vital area of a child's training, one that needs to be reinforced by family unity."

"I've already had my sermon for today, Mr. Winter."

"I didn't mean to preach. I take the blame for this," he said, grasping the table as if he had to hold on to something. "I asked Aunt Tess not to push you, feeling you needed this time to get adjusted."

"Well, Mr. Winter," Norah insisted, "I feel that the best adjustment one can make is to become part of a church where there are other caring Christians. Camille already notices everything around her. You saw that yourself today. I want her to grow up knowing that God is an integral part of her life."

Thornton drew himself up straighter and folded his arms across his chest. "I think part of this is your rebellion against me. If you wanted this to be a family affair, you could have attended the church my family has attended for generations."

"I'll bet you even have your own pew," she snorted derisively. When his shoulders stiffened, she knew she'd struck a nerve. "But as I said, Mr. Winter, it's important to feel wanted."

They glared at each other. Finally he spoke, "Who invited you?"

"Does it matter?"

"Unmistakably!" he replied. "Who is he?"

"Who said it's a he?"

"Your unwillingness to give a name," he retorted.

Norah shook her head stubbornly. She hadn't intended to broach the subject, but now it tumbled out. "Do you intend to fill me in on the details of your relationship with Madelyn?"

"I do not," he said firmly.

"Then don't expect me to divulge my every move. I have a right to a private life, too."

"That's where you're wrong. As part of my family, I do expect you to keep everything public and aboveboard."

"But you have a private life . . . with Madelyn," she insisted.

"Madelyn has nothing to do with this. Nor am I accustomed to discussing my private life with anyone."

"You are or were . . ." Norah rose and grasped the opposite side of the table with both hands, "or are going to be . . . married to her. That makes her fair game since Camille and I are part of your family."

"Is that what you learned at church?" he blared.

That was not a denial, Norah knew. "You're not being honest with me, Mr. Winter. If you're planning to bring that obviously disturbed woman in to be your wife, then I have every right to know. You want me to leave, don't you? You've tried everything from threats to ultimatums, from charm to church. Church!" she snorted. "I can't believe you would stoop so low as to resort to arguing about church!"

Thornton's shoulders sagged and he leaned over, bracing his hands on the tabletop. "What we need to do is cool off, then we'll sit down and discuss the situation like two civilized adults."

"And what is that?" she hissed.

"Maybe I can depend upon my memory!" he snapped. "I used to be one!" He turned and strode toward the house.

"Oh!" Norah gasped, the color high in her cheeks. "I think

you've *always* been one!" she yelled to his retreating figure.

He glanced over his shoulder. "Twenty years?" he called back. "Of this?" He wouldn't let her see his grin. This was more exhilarating than a run on the beach.

She stomped along behind him. "If you don't like it, you can . . . leave!"

He flung open the glass doors. Eloise was folding soft baby blankets. "Will you want supper soon?" she asked.

"Bread and water for her!" He pointed to an indignant Norah.

Norah suddenly realized he was not angry. When had it changed? The infuriating man was like a southern storm. You never knew just when it would strike, but it was inevitable.

"Well, I can cook my own," she scoffed, going along with his game. "I learned when I was six years old—seawater, sand cakes, and grass a-pair-spe-gus."

For an instant, Thornton seemed bewildered, then he threw back his head and laughed.

"And Thornton's favorite was mac-a-blony," Eloise added, joining in their laughter as she took the stack of blankets toward the bedroom.

They looked at each other. "I'm sorry," Thornton said.

Norah sank down on the couch and sighed heavily. "Since I met you, I feel as if I've been through a divorce, complete with marital discord and custody fight, and all without the benefits of marriage."

He quirked a brow meaningfully.

"Oh, Thornton," she said suddenly, "we're never going to get along long enough to bring up a child."

"Of course we are," he countered, sitting down in a chair opposite her. "We can work at it. Remember, you promised me twenty years."

She smiled. He was trying to make up for his snide remark earlier. Then he suddenly grew serious again. "We have to talk about where we go from here. And we must consider the fact that you may someday want to marry, Norah, when you find the right man."

"That's easy," she quipped. "He would have to be as dedicated to Camille's welfare as I."

Norah caught her breath as he stared intently at her. "My experience has taught me that it is not so easy to find a mate who wants to be responsible for someone else's child. When one has a child to consider, one's social life is greatly limited."

"Limited?" She laughed, hoping to steer the conversation into less troubled waters. "Why, Thornton, this past week Camille and I watched 'Sesame Street' together, read several old favorites, and went for a stroll in the fresh air nearly every day. I'd say my social life has improved considerably."

His expression grew pensive. "Do you think she's too young for *Br'er Rabbit?*"

"Not at all," Norah replied, hiding a grin.

"I almost wore the tar off that baby," he reminisced. "It was my favorite."

They laughed together. Then Norah sobered. "I want to start reading Bible stories to her at night, so that can be the last thing on her mind before she goes to sleep."

He nodded. "We can do that together."

"I want to expose her to all the most important things from the very beginning."

"I quite agree," Thornton said. "Including the values I mentioned to you in Florida, values I . . . erroneously . . . assumed you did not share."

Norah felt breathless. He approved of her?

"Norah," he said, his deep voice low and husky, "I know some fathers who have raised daughters without mothers, and the relationships were quite remarkably stable. It isn't ideal, of course, but it can be done. I never came close to replacing Mother in Chris' life, for example, but we had to deal with the reality as we found it. There are things I can't do for Camille as well as you, and vice versa. But I'll do my best."

"And I'll have to learn as I go along." Her eyes flashed. "But I would like to be able to make some of the decisions where she's concerned."

He arched a brow. "Decisions? Didn't you request swimming lessons for Camille, and didn't I go along with the idea?"

"Oh, I meant to tell you," she said, her voice rising with excitement. "The literature from the hospital came in the mail last week, and Camille and I have been practicing. I think we're ready now. I could call the instructor to come out anytime. What about tomorrow?"

"Fine!" he said with enthusiasm as Eloise entered the room. "I have some calls to make after dinner. Then we'll spend this evening making plans."

Thornton walked over to the sliding doors and looked out. How different this scene was from just two weeks ago! A placid pool beneath a serene sky, feathery clouds floating above. A quiet garden. The relaxing, rhythmic sound of the sea on a tranquil afternoon.

His peaceful haven would never be the same. The spotless deck was now strewn with toys, a baby blanket, a half-empty bottle. Baby cries and lullabies disturbed the utter stillness. The thought, "The Lord gives and the Lord takes away," drifted across his mind. Those he had lost could not be replaced. But his family could expand. Camille was an extension of them all, a part of himself.

Thank You, Lord, he breathed silently.

And that young woman, who had lain on her back, taking pictures of the sky! Just where did she fit into the scheme of things? Ah, but that was the challenge.

He realized he was smiling. It had been much too long since he had smiled or laughed . . . or argued with anyone. It felt good, invigorating.

He shook his head. *Twenty years?*

Then he noticed the novel lying on the table where Norah had set it aside and went outside to bring it in. A frown touched his lips. Josh Logan had given it to her. Wanted him to read it. And what did this Josh know about Thornton Winter?

nine

"I've changed my mind!" Thornton exclaimed, pausing long enough to glare at Norah as she undressed Camille down to her diaper. "I don't know how I could have let you talk me into this!"

Aunt Tess sat anxiously in a chair drawn up close to the pool, holding the soft blanket she would wrap the baby in after her first swimming lesson. Eloise and Henry, looking dubious, stood nearby with their arms around each other for support, while Thornton paced alongside the pool.

"Let's just listen to what the instructor has to say," Norah implored, refusing to admit that she felt a little uneasy herself. Willing to give it a try, however, she handed Camille to Thornton and sat on the side of the pool, dangling her feet in the water.

The instructor, a pretty young woman named Paula, reminded Norah of Liza Minnelli with her alert dark eyes and short black hair. Her tall, athletic build was proof that she was physically capable of handling not only babies, but grownups.

Paula's vita had been mailed to Norah, along with an instruction sheet for preparing the baby for this day. She knew that Mr. Winter had checked with the hospital, confirming her credentials. However, observing the apprehensive group huddled around the pool, she restated her qualifications that included life-saving courses, education in physical therapy, employment with the hospital for over a year, and occasional private lessons, usually with recovering patients.

No doubt Thornton was a heavy contributor to the hospital, Norah thought, to have persuaded them to send such a well-qualified instructor to teach one small child!

"It's really quite simple," Paula assured her doubtful audience. "You have been preparing the baby according to the instructions I sent?" she asked, turning to Norah.

Norah nodded. She had been blowing in Camille's face several times a day for the past few days, getting her to accept the exercise as a playful antic.

"Now," Paula said, going to the edge and slipping into the water, "after she comes up, praise her. Let her know she has done well."

Thornton's face clouded over. "Sounds like you're training a—a dog!" he objected. "This is my *niece!*"

Norah turned her face up to his. "This could save her life, Thornton . . . not only in the pool, but in the bathtub. And before long, she'll be out here in her walker."

"Not unattended, I can assure you!"

Paula spoke confidently. "This is not a measure to replace the vigilant supervision of children. Accidents can happen . . . even while you're watching."

He wasn't convinced. "She's so young and helpless."

Norah agreed. "That's exactly why it's so important," she said quietly. "Let's get started."

Thornton shrugged in resignation, and seeing that he was not going to interfere, Paula stepped forward. "Since mothers are better at this than fathers," she said to Norah, "you get into the pool."

Norah slid off the side and into the water. In spite of the reluctance and warning in his eyes, Thornton placed Camille in her arms.

Paula continued her explanation. "Now I'll blow in her face, and she will inhale sharply. That's when she should be submerged. Later, you will watch for air bubbles as she exhales. But in this beginning stage, we're only acclimating her to the water and overcoming any fear she might have. Give her to me, please."

Norah bravely handed over the baby.

Paula held Camille under her arms, facing her. The child was especially squirmy, perhaps picking up on the tension around her, and started to cry.

Before anyone could object, Paula blew into her mouth and nose. Camille gasped, halting her crying, and the entire family held its breath as Paula dunked her and held her under for a couple of seconds before bringing her up. Startled by the suddenness of the movements and the water streaming down her face, Camille cried out. Paula put her into Norah's waiting arms, and Norah comforted her, making soothing sounds.

"It's not working," Thornton declared.

"On the contrary, it worked perfectly," Paula said. "Camille will soon learn that blowing is the signal that she's going underwater. Later, she will automatically hold her breath."

Camille had quieted by now and Paula encouraged Norah, "Now you try it."

Norah took her position in the water and blew in Camille's face. The baby held her breath, and Norah dunked her and quickly brought her up. Once again, Camille sputtered in protest, but not as vigorously as before.

"That's it for today," Paula said, to the immense relief of the onlookers, who applauded and cheered this announcement.

Norah held Camille up to Thornton, and Aunt Tess bundled her in the warm blanket and crooned soothingly, praising her for her morning's work.

"I'll give her her bath." Eloise took the baby, and the little entourage disappeared inside, leaving Henry to drive Paula back to the dock after she had changed.

Norah hoisted herself to the side of the pool and cocked her head at Thornton. "Well?" she said with a triumphant grin. "What do you think? Don't you agree that I was right?"

"Absolutely!" he declared, kneeling down beside her.

"*Everyone* should be subjected to such treatment." With that, through open lips he drew in a deep breath, expanding his chest. The wicked gleam in his eyes was unmistakable.

"You wouldn't dare!" she squealed, and to escape, she jumped into the pool, splashing him in the process.

He flinched, warding off the rain of drops. Resisting the impulse to retaliate instantly, he sat on the edge of the pool and eased his feet into the water, speaking quietly, "I can tell she's going to be a championship swimmer."

Norah bobbed in the water, dog paddling. "So, you have to admit I was right about this one!"

"You? You can't take the credit. Remember, you can't do a thing without my permission." When she opened her mouth to retort, he suddenly drew up his knees, then forced his feet into the water, making a trememdous splash.

He had intended to jump up from the side, but she was too quick. Ducking beneath the surface, she came up with her body and her arms, flinging the water at him, dousing him, and creating a stream that ran onto the deck.

Getting to his feet awkwardly, arms outstretched, he scowled at her, water dripping from his hair and down his face.

Norah chortled with glee. "You look like you did the night the hurricane blew you into Florida."

At the memory, the laughter died in her throat. That night she had been so afraid he'd take Camille from her. Now she was freely offering to share Camille with him. Had he changed so drastically? Or had she? Panic washed over her like a wave. With a thundering heart, she turned in the water and swam to the other side of the pool.

Thornton reached for a towel from a table and began drying himself. He'd seen the playful challenge in her eyes turn to doubt. Or was it fear? Was she disappointed that he hadn't risen to her challenge? Or was she afraid he might? Still, he didn't want to leave her out here alone, while the family was inside, gloating over Camille's momentous accomplishment.

"Norah," he called, when she reached the other side, "let's go in." He held out his hand toward her.

Skeptical all the way, she swam toward him. At the edge, she looked up at him. It wasn't a game any more. She shook her head.

"Trust me."

Norah lifted herself out of the pool and hesitantly took his outstretched hand. He pulled her up and handed her a towel.

Stunned by his gallant gesture, she could only stare into his face, his lips lifted in a dazzling smile. "Thank you," she murmured.

As she was toweling off, an old saying came to mind: "The only thing we have to fear is fear itself." Surely she didn't have anything to fear from this gentle man.

Did she?

❧

How could she have possibly imagined that her decision to share Camille with Thornton Winter would solve their problems? Norah wondered. Their discussions about what was best for Lantz's child had quickly escalated to a total rehash of all the pros and cons she and Thornton had ever fought about. Only this time, it was being accompanied by the legal advice of experts—*Thornton's* paid experts!

Now they were sitting at the dining room table while John Grimes, the senior attorney, made notes to include in his petition to present to a judge.

"Filing for joint custody is the only way to ensure Camille's welfare," he had said, persuading her at last that it was true. And today, he went one step further as he warned, "Of course, there's always the chance that a judge might not award joint custody, but possibly will want to decide which of you should get full custody."

"But we're not divorced!" Norah protested, distressed at the prospect. "We don't want to divide Camille. We want to share her!"

"But if you two can't decide what's best," John informed her, "then there's the danger of Camille becoming a ward of the court until you can come to some kind of agreement."

That would be worse. Instead of the two of them making a decision, it would be made by an objective, unemotional third party.

"Let's try to work together," she pleaded.

"Good," John said. "Now, here's what you must do. Keep all emotions under control and think only of the baby. You must convince a judge that you're not fighting for separate custody, but that you want to share."

By Friday, John Grimes had written up the presentation he would make to a judge and, when Thornton hand-delivered a copy to Norah, she sat down and read it immediately. The document dealt only with their intentions and not with their doubts and frustrations. But John Grimes was Thornton Winter's legal representative, paid to act in his behalf, and Norah still wasn't sure she was being fairly represented.

What other recourse did she have? she fretted silently. She did want to share Camille with Thornton Winter. She did want the security for the baby that he offered. And to fight Thornton in court would be much more painful than a few discourses in the dining room at the beach house.

"What do you think?" Thornton asked after she'd read it.

"On paper, it sounds fair," she said. "But it's not so simple. Nothing is really settled—only delayed."

"Things, and people, change, Norah. A judge will have to take that into consideration."

"I know. It's just that I'm not sure any more what's right. I need to get away and think. I'm in your house, listening to your family, your attorneys. I need an objective opinion."

"You want another attorney?"

"Shouldn't I have my own? You pay John and his assistant to represent your best interests."

He shrugged. "That's your prerogative. Shall I suggest someone?"

"No," she said offhandedly, "I'll find someone."

"Then go ahead," he said stiffly. His eyes fell on the novel lying on the edge of the bar. He could see that the card being used as a marker was a personal business card. "You intend to call Josh, don't you?"

She shrugged. "So? What did you expect? Did you think I would open the phone book and pick a name at random over something this important?"

"All right," he said. "I have no objections."

While Norah left to make her call in the privacy of the library, Thornton picked up the book and flipped it over. On the back cover, where the critics were quoted, he read: "A penetrating, thought-provoking saga of unselfish love to rival the wisdom of King Solomon in the case of the divided child."

He looked out toward the palms, swaying in the morning breeze, and searched his memory for the familiar Bible story. Two women, who had laid claim to a baby, had sought the judgment of wise King Solomon. When Solomon suggested dividing the child with a sword, giving half to each woman, the real mother had spoken up in alarm. "Give the child to her!" she had cried, thus proving a real mother's love.

Thornton shook his head in denial. That plot did not fit their situation. Neither he nor Norah was trying to divide Camille. Nor did they want to fight over her. They simply wanted to share her.

Who did this Josh think he was? Some young whippersnapper who had gotten all starry-eyed over Norah and was trying to tell her how to run her life? He didn't care for outside interference in his family. And Norah was family, at least for now.

He looked up as she came back into the room. "I'd like to go out for a while tonight, if that's all right," she said, expecting an argument.

But there was none. "Fine. I'll be with Camille. But I need to be away tomorrow afternoon and evening, possibly quite late." He regarded her silently for a moment. "I can be reached at Madelyn's."

He had hoped she might reveal her own whereabouts, but when she didn't, he said, "Come on. I'll drive you to the ferry."

*

"Why are you doing this?" she asked Thornton later as he drove onto the ferry instead of letting her out.

"Because I'm a gentleman."

"The real reason," she probed.

"You'll see when we get there," he said to her in exasperation.

"It's only Josh," she confessed on the way. "I have no other friends here."

"I suppose you've told him about the baby."

"He's the one who took me to check out the nursery at church. There he is now," she said, spotting Josh as the ferry pulled into the dock. He was leaning up against his red sports car, waiting for her.

Thornton wheeled the Mercedes into the slot beside him and killed the engine. Getting out, Norah introduced the two men, and Josh stuck out a big paw.

Thornton accepted his handshake tentatively. He had expected to find a much younger man, but Logan appeared to be around his own age, somewhere in his midthirties. "I want to thank you for suggesting that I read *Undivided*. Very thoughtful of you."

Josh nodded. A tense moment passed as the two men studied each other surreptitiously.

"Interesting novel," Thornton went on.

"You've read it, then?" Josh wanted to know.

"Enough to get the point. I know how it ends."

Norah looked at the two men. At Thornton's statement, Josh had appeared somewhat diminished, though he'd have to go a long way for that, she thought. Like Thornton, he was a big man, and although his heavy beard and thick hair gave him a brawny look, he had the refined muscular structure of a dancer.

Feeling the tension bristling between them, she said cheerily, "Oh, Thornton, you should never read the ending first. It ruins the story."

"You're right," he agreed, "that's exactly what happened." He smiled, but his eyes were glittering strangely. "Have a good evening," he said and, without another glance, he returned to his car and drove back onto the ferry.

"I think I touched a nerve, without meaning to," Josh said after they were in the car and buckled up.

"He's just particular about the company kept by his niece's guardian," Norah explained. "He must have approved, though, or he would have escorted me right back to the island. But he's not as gruff as he appears."

"Oh, I didn't think he was gruff." Josh gave a wry laugh. "Men who own islands just speak a different language."

"I suppose so," she agreed. "And what did he communicate to you?"

"Proceed with caution."

Norah laughed uneasily, then told him a little about her dilemma. "I'm afraid of losing Camille," she confessed, "and going before a judge seems such a drastic measure. A court will decide her future."

"Do you have any recourse?" Josh asked.

"Not unless I want my parents to apply for custody. But I don't want to take Camille away from Thornton Winter. He's a fine man, Josh. Camille and he need each other. They love each other."

"I can't advise you in something this important," he said. "But since you both want to share the baby, it looks as if this is the only way, without going through a worse court battle."

"I know," she said and sighed. "But Thornton Winter has decided he will rear this child, and I have no choice but to let him, even if it means I lose control."

"You also gain some control, Norah. Being established as a legal guardian, even jointly, will give you more ammunition for what might come up later on."

"It would do the same for him," she argued.

There was a moment of silence while he contemplated the facts. "What would Camille's parents want?"

She shook her head. "Oh, Josh, they would want us both to take care of her. But even the attorney is saying a judge will probably consider the situation unstable and temporary, at best."

"And what do you think?"

"For me, it would be ideal if Camille and I could stay at the beach house, with Eloise and Henry to take care of everything, and Thornton dropping in occasionally to relate to Camille. But we have to move to town where it's convenient for him. It's scary, thinking about our living together in that house."

"Are you worried about . . . his taking advantage of you?"

"Not at all!" She laughed at the very idea. "He sees me as a female counterpart to Chris, like a sister he can parent."

Josh didn't reply that he felt Thornton Winter was more perceptive than that. "Then you might try the prayer of serenity: 'Lord, help me to change the things I can, and accept the things I cannot. And give me the wisdom to know the difference.'"

"I suppose you're right," she said and they exchanged a knowing look. "I'm helpless. I have nowhere else to turn."

Unexpectedly, Josh began to sing in his baritone voice: " 'I must tell Jesus all of my trials; I cannot bear my burdens alone. In my distress He kindly will help me. He ever loves and cares for His own. I must tell Jesus; I must tell Jesus. I cannot bear my burdens alone. I must tell Jesus; I must tell Jesus. Jesus can help me. Jesus alone.' "

Norah turned a radiant smile on Josh when he had finished. "Thanks. You have a way of helping me put things in perspective."

"Sometimes you can be too close to a situation to be objective, Norah. I was so bent on finding my sister's murderer that I was completely frustrated when God didn't open up a job for me in North Carolina so I could pursue the case. I couldn't see that He was answering my prayer by giving me eight years in Charleston to gain distance and perspective. Now I can return with a clear head, instead of wanting to kill somebody myself!" He shook his head. "We don't   always know what's best for us, Norah, but if we seek God's will, He works out a plan for us that beats anything we could think up on our own."

"Are you saying you think a period of temporary custody would give me time to gain perspective?"

"I don't want to influence any decision you make, Norah. I can only speak from my own experience."

"Would you mind reading what the attorney will present to the judge," she asked hesitantly, then tried to make a joke of it, "since an eligible bachelor like you has nothing better to do on a beautiful spring evening?"

He grinned at her. "You're right, I don't. It's been pretty hectic for the past few years, but things are winding down now. Besides, I can't think of anyone I'd rather spend this evening with."

She flashed him a grateful smile. "I really appreciate this, Josh."

He glanced over at her as he pulled in at The Trawler, then parked and turned to face her. "If you recall, Norah, the first day we met, I offered my friendship. I knew then . . . well, you know what would settle this whole thing, don't you?"

She winced. "Only in my fantasy!" she said. "But, Josh, that's an impossible dream. About as likely as Scarlett marrying Rhett."

"Have you read the sequel?" he asked.

"No," she admitted.

"Neither have I. So, the ending is up for grabs, isn't it?" He grinned again, showing his white teeth. "Come on. Let's go in. We'll talk and eat and I'll read your papers."

After he read them, he agreed they sounded like the ideal solution for two people intent upon putting a child's best interest first, even above their own. "But that's looking at it unemotionally, Norah," he said. "I can't tell you what your ultimate decision must be. Just consider your options, pray about it, and act according to your best judgment."

ᴥ

Thornton left early Saturday, saying he had appointments to keep. He called late Saturday night to ask Norah if she'd like him or Aunt Tess to meet her and Camille at the dock and take them to his church. She declined.

Instead, on Sunday morning, she left Camille with Eloise, asked Henry to drive her to the ferry, where Josh met her and took her to his church. It was after church that Thornton called again. "I'll be home this afternoon," he said. "We'll have supper, and after Camille is settled for the night, I'd like to take you someplace."

"Where?" she asked, but he wouldn't say.

"Just dress casually. And wear low-heeled shoes."

ten

Casual, Thornton had said.

Norah grimaced at her reflection in the mirror. Any time she and Thornton Winter spent more than a few minutes together, it was anything but casual!

Nevertheless, she had chosen one of her own outfits instead of Hillary's—a floral print of yellow and pink roses with deep green leaves against a white background. The circle skirt fell to mid-calf; the halter top had an elasticized back and a scooped neckline. That left her shoulders bare, but her hair would cover them.

She suspected he preferred her hair loose and unconfined, so she brushed it out and let it curl freely around her face. The sun had enlivened the copper-colored spirals with a golden sheen.

She spent a little more time than usual with her makeup, enhancing her eyes with a subtle shadow and touching her lips with a dewy rose-colored gloss.

When she was done, she almost stepped into high heels before she remembered he'd specified low-heeled shoes. What, she wondered, did he have in mind? A tearose crocheted lace flat that she sometimes wore as houseslippers would do nicely.

While fastening a gold loop earring in her earlobe and seeing the expectation in the reflection of her green eyes, she reminded herself that this was not a date. Thornton had just spent a weekend, or part of it, with Madelyn.

A kind of dread seized her. Was he going to soften her up, then present yet another demand? Sighing, she breathed a little prayer and stepped into the game room.

Waiting for her was not the aloof, formal, scowling man in a conservative business suit. Instead, Thornton was wearing a white shirt striped in blue that complemented the silver at his temples and made his eyes appear lighter. He looked incredibly young and fresh. He was sitting on the couch, reading the book Josh had given her, swinging his socked foot for Camille's amusement. The baby lay on a quilt on the floor, turning her head to follow the motion of his foot.

At Norah's approach, Thornton recovered his shoe and got to his feet, looking her over with appreciation, then glancing down. "Good, I see you're wearing sensible shoes." Then he knelt and kissed Camille's head. "Be a sweet girl for Eloise, now."

In the car on the way to the ferry, they commented on the perfect weather. The sun was a golden ball sinking into the sea. Dusk shimmered with a fiery incandescence, either from the retreating sun or the rising moon.

At the dock, there was a surprise for Norah in the garage. "My Rabbit!" she squealed, feeling as if she were seeing an old friend, one who had apparently had a facelift.

"You might want to rename it," he said playfully, holding out a set of keys. "I'm told it no longer hops, skips, and jumps, but purrs like a kitten. But we won't find out tonight. This is my treat. We go in my car."

She slid the keys into her purse and got back into the Mercedes. "Thank you, Thornton, for going to all that trouble. And as soon as you give me the bill, I'll repay you."

"Not that again!" There was an edge to his voice. "Can't you just accept a little Southern hospitality without having to feel obligated?"

She kept quiet for the entire ferry ride. It was only after they had left the ferry and had driven through Mt. Pleasant, across a drawbridge, and onto the Cooper River Bridge toward the historic district, that Thornton broke the long silence.

"This place is a paradox," he said. "On one hand, it's a growing, thriving, modern city, but it's also a fascinating port that has preserved its history. Instead of just reading about it in the history books, you can walk through streets, homes, and gardens that are still virtually the same as they were in the mid-1600's."

After he parked on a side street, Thornton led her around a corner and Norah felt as if she had stepped into another world. Horse-drawn carriages rolled along cobblestone streets. Grand houses, reminiscent of the 18th and 19th centuries, adorned with piazzas and shutters, were guarded by lacy iron fences. Her eyes widened when Thornton pointed out Rainbow Row, an entire block of homes that looked like pastel dollhouses.

"I'm beginning to understand why you've found the past so enchanting," she breathed, looking about her with awe.

Yes, Thornton thought, as he led Norah along The Battery, *enchanting is the word for her.*

They stood at the seawall and looked out over the harbor. "There's Fort Sumter," he said.

"Where?" Her gaze swept the watery expanse. She felt the strong bulk of Thornton's body as he pulled her to his side, encircling her shoulders with his muscular arm.

He pointed out over the churning sea, lapping at the concrete seawall. "There," he said, as if she could see more than lights far across the water. "That's where the War Between the States began, about 150 years ago."

Her bare shoulder, cool and soft, grew warm beneath his hand, and the sea breeze lifted her hair and trailed it along his arm. They talked on about this and that, their conversation blending with the rhythmic sound of the sea.

Thornton knew the instant Norah became uncomfortable with his arm about her. Her questioning glance barely met his and she grew quiet. He moved his arm away.

They walked on through White Point Gardens. She laughed

lightly when he had to dislodge a piece of lacy moss that caught in her hair as she passed under a great live oak. "Pirates once dangled from the gallows here," he said and watched her squirm.

He was enjoying introducing Norah to Charleston, his home. Seeing it through her shining eyes, he felt anew the allure of the old city. Her remarks, once so hostile toward the town he loved so much, were now filled with exclamations of delight.

On the way to the tour houses, he pointed out Catfish Row that had inspired the opera "Porgy & Bess" and the Four Corners of Law, an intersection with buildings representing municipal, county, federal, and God's law.

The streets were crowded with people of varying nationalities and economic levels. Some were in groups, being led by tour guides along sidewalks lighted by candles in paper bags, half filled with sand, to denote the path.

"Oh, it's like Christmas, complete with wooden soldiers!" Norah said, referring to the uniformed guards who stood outside the homes.

"Citadel cadets," Thornton explained. "Chris might even be around here somewhere."

A young couple stood looking at a map, wondering aloud, "Where is Calhoun Mansion?"

Overhearing them, Thornton stopped to say, "That's where we're going. Why don't you just follow us?"

"Are you a tour guide?" the young man asked.

"Tonight, I am," Thornton replied enigmatically, noting Norah's look of surprise. He held her hand to keep them together as a wave of sightseers surged around them and passed by.

"Incidentally," Thornton said to the young couple, as they neared Calhoun Mansion, "you'll find the gardens at the mansion particularly interesting. They've been beautifully restored."

They listened intently, as Thornton sketched the history of the estate and moved over as curious passersby joined the group. "The house was built after the Civil War by the wealthy merchant and banker, George Walton Williams."

"What kind of architecture?" asked someone in the crowd.

"It's a Victorian Baronial Manor House, built in 1876, with 24,000 square feet, a stairwell that rises to a 75-foot domed ceiling, and a ballroom with a coved glass skylight. The ceilings are 14 feet high, and the house boasts elaborate chandeliers and ornate plaster and wood moldings."

At his smug look, Norah cast him a sidelong glance and whispered loudly, "Is this your home, Thorn, the one you said was on the historic list?"

"Not so loud," he muttered under his breath.

"Well, you told me you owned one of these mansions," she sweetly persisted.

He scowled ominously. Those who had been following him, hanging on to every word, now peered at him with even greater interest.

As they were walking out, the young man asked, "Do you really live in one of these mansions?"

Thornton shrugged casually. "Mine's just a shack compared with the Calhoun Mansion, but it's near here. *She* lives out by the ocean," he said, motioning to Norah. "Now there's a different kind of experience. You can get a glimpse of the house from the beach at Seabreeze Island, and it's free!"

"Hey, thanks for telling us. We might just do that." The young man reached for his companion's hand and they slipped away.

"Which one is yours, Thornton?" Norah asked when they were outside and had joined up with a group led by a paid tour guide.

"We'll see if you can guess."

As they neared the next house on the tour, the guide began

to explain. "This lovely old mansion is in the Greek Revival style and is characteristic of those built in Ansonborough after the disastrous fire of 1838."

"What was that?" Norah whispered.

"Sh," he reprimanded. "You're not interested in history, remember?"

When the group started inside, Thornton pointed out to Norah the ironwork that surrounded the house, extending to the garden in the back. An iron railing bordered the steps and the colonnaded porch, and there were second- and third-floor balconies across the entire front of the house. They slipped into the living room behind the others just as the guide began to speak again.

"The owners of this house died in a tragic accident and passed the house down to the present owner, a leading designer, builder, and renovator, the renowned Mr. Thornton T. Winter."

Thornton leaned down and spoke in a whisper, "Probably some old stuffed shirt."

Norah stifled a giggle and looked around. The entry boasted a wide center hall and an elegant staircase that was roped off by a red velvet cord. There was an aura of grandeur and formality, enhanced by the high ceilings, long narrow windows, elegant furnishings, and gleaming antiques. Every room boasted a fireplace.

Along the right side of the house was the living room, a bedroom, and kitchen. Along the left was the parlor, library, and the dining room. "The hall extends to a back entry where stairs lead to a private garden," the guide told them. On the two floors above them, the arrangement of rooms was similar to the first.

"The current owner lives here during the off season," the guide told the crowd, and Norah was reminded that this magnificent house would soon be her new home.

When the tour ended, Thornton lagged behind, eager to learn Norah's reaction. "You don't like it," he said, unable to read her veiled expression.

"Of course I like it," she contradicted. "It's grand and beautiful, and . . ." she wailed, "I'd be afraid to move or sit on the furniture."

His face clouded. "Norah, you sit on it just like you sit on the wicker furniture at the beach house. Or on the sand. Or the floor."

"It's no place for a baby," she said. "Have you ever seen a baby fly through a house in a walker with rollers on it?"

"You forget that I was brought up here. We didn't have walkers in my day, but I was fourteen when Chris was born, so I remember his childhood well. Haven't you heard the expression, 'If you can't keep the child away from the antique, keep the antique away from the child'?"

"In my part of the world, the word was *temptation*, not *antique*," Norah said and laughed lightly.

As they stepped outside, a voice spoke out of the darkness, "Is there a problem, ma'am?"

Norah spun around. "Chris!" she exclaimed. "I didn't see you there."

He walked up onto the porch. "I had orders to stay out of sight until after you'd seen the house."

"Well, she hasn't seen the house yet, Chris. We're going back in," Thornton explained sternly.

"Sorry, *sir*," Chris said in a military monotone. "That's not allowed after the tour has ended. You make such an attempt, and I'll have to report you to the authorities."

Norah tried to suppress her laughter, while Thornton glared.

"Those are my orders, *sir*," Chris continued staunchly. "A Citadel man and a Winter man never disobeys orders, *sir*."

"You don't take bribes either, do you?" Thornton asked.

"Not unless it's a white Mercedes, *sir*!" Chris shouted, standing at attention.

"Suppose you don't get permission for any more weekend leaves?"

"You win, *sir*," Chris returned and cut his eyes around at his brother.

"Come on," Thornton said to Norah, giving Chris a good-natured jab as he passed.

Thornton unlocked the door and they stepped into the silent house. Moonlight filtered through the long narrow windows, casting elongated shadows across the floor. Taking her hand, he led her over to the staircase and flipped a switch that lighted a chandelier suspended from the high ceiling above the stairs. He let go of her hand, unhooked the velvet cord, and turned toward her.

This was where Rhett swooped Scarlett up in his arms and raced up the stairs, Norah dreamed. A wicked gleam appeared in Thornton's eyes but died instantly, and he was once again the dignified master of the house, leading the way to the second floor.

"This floor will belong to you and Camille," he said, as he opened a door to an empty room. "The nursery here adjoins your bedroom."

They walked through the empty room and into a bedroom that looked and smelled of polished wood. Norah touched the motif of the bed's carved footposts. Seeing her interest, Thornton explained, "This is an 1800's Charleston-made rice bed."

She followed as he walked across the wool rug onto a dark hardwood floor, past gracefully curved tapestry chairs, by an antique desk, and into an elegant sitting room.

"These were Lantz's rooms," Thornton explained. "If you want anything changed before you move in, just say so. We've moved Chris to the third floor."

"Does he mind?" Norah asked quickly.

"He's delighted," Thornton replied. "The studio is on that floor where the lighting is better. He'll be working with me during the summer, along with creating his own designs."

Norah realized anew how creative this family was, how conscientious. "I wonder what Camille will be when she grows up?" she said reflectively.

"Probably Madam President. Already she exhibits characteristics of being strong-willed and intelligent, not to mention that she's a flaming-haired beauty." He laughed and led the way into the hall.

Norah laughed with him and followed him down the stairs. With each minute, each day, she gained a better understanding of why Lantz had asked Thornton to take care of his child. How selfish it would be of her to deny Camille the opportunity to grow up under the Winter influence.

"Aunt Tess has volunteered to stay here at night, if you'd feel better," he said. "She can take one of the rooms on second. Hilda comes every day and stays overnight whenever she wants. Her rooms are on the basement floor."

At the bottom of the stairs, Norah's eyes swept toward the parlor on the left, the living room on the right. "It's a lovely home."

"Thank you," he said simply. "Now, let me show you where you'll be working."

"Working?"

He grinned. "Weren't you the one who insisted on paying her own way?"

Feeling lighthearted, Norah followed him into the library, where he switched on the light. On the earlier tour, she had been impressed by the two walls of mahogany bookshelves reaching from floor to ceiling. A huge mahogany desk dominated the room, positioned in front of cabinets where Thornton kept sketching supplies. In the center of the outside wall was a brick fireplace with two chairs pulled up in front.

A silver frame on the desk caught Norah's eye. She walked over and picked it up. "What is this?" she asked, puzzled, turning it sideways, then upside down.

"A conversation piece, you might say," Thornton replied in an offhanded manner.

Norah glanced at him skeptically, then squinted. "Of course," she said, "it's a picture of the emperor's new clothes!"

Thornton's short laugh quickly subsided, and Norah noticed the guarded look that came into his eyes. He stood stiffly erect, his fingers touching the desk, some dark thought shadowing his face.

Norah lowered her gaze to the picture frame. A conversation piece, he'd said. In the silence, the part of her that sensed and responded to the deeper concerns of a hurting human being longed to reach out to him, to ask him what had caused that sudden withdrawal into himself. But how? "I don't hear any conversation," she quipped.

"You're making too much of this," Thornton said with irritation. "It's only an empty frame. I used to put sketches of a dream house in there as it developed. Then one day the dream vanished. The sketches have been . . . burned. But," he said abruptly, moving toward the door, "enough of that. Let's go." He switched off the light.

The glow from the upstairs chandelier silhouetted his tall frame in the doorway and sent a long shadow across the floor.

"Do you know when is the best time to answer a child's questions?" Norah flung across the dark gulf now separating them. When he made no response, she answered her own question, "When they ask."

"Forever the psychologist, aren't you?" he scoffed.

"You said I was family," she returned, having learned that his gruffness was a façade, a coverup for some pain in his heart. She wanted to know—needed to know—what that was. Risking his displeasure, she walked over to the nearest chair and sat down.

Yes, he thought to himself, as Camille's blood relative, Norah was family. But she was also strong-willed, independent, stubborn—very much her own appealing person. Theirs was a relationship they'd have to discuss. He hadn't intended it to be tonight, but the carefree mood of earlier evening was gone. He would have to tell her his . . . intentions for the future. And the best way might be to preface them with a brief sketch of his own past.

"I've never had a sister before," he said, turning back into the shadowed room.

"And I've never had a brother," she said, "but I guess it's sort of like having a sister."

"And how was that?"

Norah thought. "In difficult times we stuck together like glue. In good times we fought like . . ." She paused, seeing him perch on the edge of the desk, arms folded over his chest.

"Like my brothers and I," he finished. "Primarily Lantz. We were close, but he was headstrong, belligerent, wouldn't listen to anyone."

Norah suppressed a smile. Thornton could very well be describing himself. Lantz, compared with Thornton, was only a mild breeze.

He picked up the empty picture frame and stared at it. Norah waited in suspense, reminding herself that she should not feel disappointed, but elated that he was willing to talk to her like a sister.

"Norah," he said into the dimness, "that first night, you talked about children needing more than material things. Well, so do adults." His eyes swept the room. "People from all over the world come to see this house, to admire it, maybe to wish they could live in one like it." He spoke gravely, "But for the past two years, the worst days of my life have been spent here."

Norah caught the flicker of anguish in his eyes before he

quickly concealed it. "Madelyn and I were engaged," he said, staring at the frame, seeing his own life unfold. "Her parents and mine were friends. For years, she was of no particular concern of mine. I was getting out of college by the time she was entering. There were plenty of females around in those days, and Winter men are traditionally career-oriented and don't marry until we're well established in careers."

"They don't . . . fall in love?" she asked, incredulous.

He gave a wry smile. "I'm not one to think of love as something so trivial as butterflies and bells. Love, to me, involves far more than fluttery feelings. I think of love as a design that begins with a few lines on paper, then grows and develops . . . sometimes quickly, sometimes very slowly. And sometimes . . .," he said, setting the empty frame on the desk, "the sketches don't work."

He went over to sit in the chair opposite her. "Anyway," he said, resuming his story, "the death of my parents put everything on hold for me for a while. Later, Chris finished high school and Lantz was into his acting career. Madelyn came home from Paris, having just broken off an engagement, her third. But that didn't concern me unduly. She was in her late twenties, quite beautiful, and we seemed to have much in common."

Thornton paused, staring at Norah in the dim light, as if seeing her for the first time.

"Wh—what?" she asked uneasily.

"Just a thought," he said. Tradition, family background, financial and historic ties to Charleston—these were the common roots that bound him to Madelyn. On the other hand, despite her youth, Norah possessed many remarkable Christian virtues—deep conviction, responsibility, loyalty, self-sacrifice, a giving spirit. Had this been what Lantz meant when he'd said they had something in common?

Norah dared not move, dared not venture a question, but

waited for Thornton to continue.

"We began seeing each other," he said, taking up the story. "All things considered, it seemed right that we should marry. She accepted my ring. The engagement was announced in the paper." He paused and drew a deep breath. "Lantz came home for the engagement party."

Norah closed her eyes. She could guess the rest.

"I don't know exactly when it started, but I do know the attraction was instant and . . . mutual. I tried to dismiss it. Most men would find her attractive. And women had always been drawn to Lantz."

He looked over at Norah and she met his steady gaze. *Not I,* she was thinking. He looked again into the dark gaping hole of the fireplace. "Madelyn was older than Lantz, however, and she was engaged to me. I was his brother, his guardian. I can't fault anyone for honest emotion. However, I did expect better than I received from these two people who claimed to love me."

"Are you sure . . .?"

"Oh, yes," he interrupted before she could finish the thought. "I found out in a most dramatic way after Lantz told Madelyn it was over: that he had found someone else, whom I now know was your sister."

"You must have been heartbroken," she said.

"No," he said brusquely. "I would have been heartbroken if they had come to me, confessed honestly that they were in love and wanted to break the engagement." He shook his head sadly. "But she wore my ring the entire time she was seeing Lantz. I was not heartbroken. I was . . ." He searched for a word, "furious! Outraged!"

"Did you try to . . . harm her?" Norah asked, her heart in her mouth.

Thornton bent his head and, for one brief moment, she suspected he was crying. Then he lifted his head and laughed.

"No, it was the other way around. *She* almost killed *me* . . . in an automobile accident." He waved his hand in dismissal. "It's a long story."

He got up and walked over to the desk again, his back to her, gazing at the picture frame. "I was sketching a home for her. I felt that a house should be built around a family, instead of fitting a family into a house." Then he turned to face her. "In the hospital, Lantz asked me to forgive him."

"And did you?"

"I said the words." He looked up toward the tall ceiling. "It's not that easy, but I think I'm getting close."

"And did Madelyn ask for your forgiveness?"

"A hundred times or more," he said distantly.

Norah felt he'd entered another world. The room suddenly seemed so dark and chilly. How could they have done that to him? How could he stand it? Was he in the process of forgiving Madelyn now? Did he still love her and want her back?

Norah rose and walked to the window, where soft moonlight filtered through. Perhaps it would warm the chill she felt inside.

"Now I've spoiled our evening, haven't I?" Thornton apologized, walking over to stand beside her.

"No, I wanted to know so I could understand."

"And do you?" he asked softly.

"No." She felt the stirrings of anger as she looked into his face. "I don't understand how they could do that to you! I don't understand how any woman would choose Lantz over *you*!" She caught her breath, horrified at her admission.

She heard his intake of breath, saw his lips parted slightly. Didn't he know that Madelyn wasn't right for him? She'd hurt him so deeply, far deeper than a cut on the face.

"Oh, Thornton," she whispered as she brought her hand to his cheek, and before she could say more, he spoke in a warning tone, "Norah, don't," and even as she lifted her lips to his wounded face, he was saying, "Don't do this, Norah."

She didn't listen. He felt the velvet smoothness of her lips, like a healing balm, move across his cheek. Felt the soft press of her warm body against his chest, melting his frozen heart. He grasped her shoulders and held her gently away from him. Her face was turned to his, her eyes moist with caring.

"Norah," he said huskily as his head bent toward hers, drawn by the play of moonlight on her lips, "don't . . . don't let me do this."

Suddenly, caught in a powerful undertow, she felt the sand shifting beneath her feet and she was being swept away. There was no time nor space, only the impossible, wonderful feeling of Thornton Winter's arms around her, holding her close.

She swayed on the waves of emotion as his lips touched first the moonlight on her face, her eyelids, her lips—softly, gently. Her arms went around his neck and Thornton's hand wound its way through the silky strands of her hair.

"Norah, Norah . . . I didn't mean . . ." He stopped, turned from her and grasped the drapes, his chest rising with his breathing.

Why did he look at her as if he didn't know who she was? Was he thinking of Madelyn? Wishing she were in his arms? Had he intended a peck on the cheek as one might kiss a baby . . . or a sister? Norah hugged her arms to herself. She'd never be able to look at him again.

Then he reached over and touched her trembling lips with his finger. "I . . . told you not to let me kiss you." His reprimand was infinitely tender.

"Well," she said, as forcefully as she could muster, with the breath driven from her body, "don't you know that you can't tell me what to do, Thornton Winter? I . . . make my own decisions."

Lifting her chin, she turned on her heel and walked over to the chair in front of the fireplace, sinking into it. It was useless to tell her heart to be still. She felt she could understand her sister better now. How in a weak moment one could make wrong, irrevocable decisions.

Thinking of Hillary and Lantz, she spoke up. "Thornton, as I told you before, I won't submit myself to the kind of situation that my sister was in."

He turned abruptly and came to take the chair opposite her. "I wasn't suggesting that at all, Norah," he said staunchly. "Believe me. It was . . . just a kiss."

Just a kiss? Norah thought. Then it had meant nothing to him.

"Not that it wasn't wonderful, Norah. But now that you know I find you lovely and desirable, and that you respond to me, we must decide what to do about it." He rose and began to pace the floor.

Thornton knew what he had to say, regardless of his feelings. He and Norah were both vulnerable right now, could take advantage of each other and justify it on the basis of what was good for Camille. His gaze moved to the empty picture frame on the desk. He'd been fooled once. It couldn't happen again. A kiss changed nothing. He did not live his life on emotion, but logic.

"Norah," he said, beginning to present the scenario, "soon we will be living here as a family. You and I will function as parents. This will be your home as well as mine. However, our commitment is to Camille and not to each other. Your reputation is to be considered as well as my own obligations which I cannot, in all good conscience, abandon."

Norah closed her eyes as if that would prevent his saying more. But it didn't. "Therefore, I will continue seeing Madelyn, and I suggest that you make friends and pursue a personal life of your own."

Well, what did he think? That just because he had paid her a few compliments she was ready to fall at his feet? That just because he had come to her like a hurricane, churning her emotions and turning her life upside down, she had fallen in love with him? And that just because he'd kissed her, she would forever define her life on the basis of one emotionally-packed encounter in the moonlight?

Well, if so, he was right.

Never had she expected to be grateful for all those acting lessons. If actors could learn to produce tears instantly, then perhaps they could learn to hold them back. She blinked hard and reentered the world of reality.

"Have you ever been in love, Norah?"

"Almost," she whispered breathlessly, "but he was dying with leukemia. So there was nothing physical, only regret for what could never be between us." Thornton leaned over to cover her hands with his own as she continued, "It was a kind of spiritual love, I guess, deep and good and pure. Wonderful, really. But I know that was partly because it had to end." She looked at him through misty eyes.

"Here," he said, rising to pull her to her feet, "let me comfort you. Isn't that what friends are for?" She succumbed to the security of his embrace, wishing she could stay there forever. "This is what we need to be able to do, Norah. Relate to each other without being self-conscious. I want you to know that you are special to me. I . . . need you in my life."

Of course, he told himself, he needed her for Camille. What else? She made him laugh, she challenged him, she complimented him when other women thought his wound such a tragedy, and even Madelyn could not look at him without crying. Yes, he needed Norah.

He needs me, Norah thought. He needs me to care for Camille. . . . She shrugged off the thought. She didn't care. She'd never hurt him as Madelyn had, and as long as he needed her, she would be there.

"We'd better go now," Thornton whispered. But as she turned

to leave the room, he put out his hand and grasped her arm. "Wait. I think you ought to know that there will never be a repeat of what happened here tonight."

He flipped the switch that turned out the upstairs light, and they walked out into the cool, crisp night.

"And I think *you* ought to know," she said, as they walked to the car, "that I didn't hear any bells or feel any butterflies."

"Neither did I," he said blandly, then glanced up and smiled at the stars. They'd never looked so bright.

eleven

On Monday, John Grimes called to tell them that Judge Lee wanted to see the baby before making a final decision and would expect to see Thornton and Norah in her chambers the next day.

"What if the judge rules that we can't have custody?" Norah asked fearfully. "Will Camille be made a ward of the court?"

"Don't even think it," Thornton moaned.

On Tuesday morning, feeling apprehensive, the two of them were seated in Judge Lee's office with Camille looking her best in a white knit dress trimmed in pink with matching headband and wearing her first real shoes, a pair of black patent leather Mary Janes.

The judge couldn't keep her eyes off Camille and compared her with her own two children at that age, casually dropping in references to the custody hearing. It made the proceedings much easier to take, Norah thought, though as far as she could tell, everything seemed to be going in Thornton's favor. His qualifications were impeccable since he had been his brothers' guardian for the past twelve years, and everyone knew his reputation as an upstanding businessman in the community.

When Camille became restless and began to whimper, Thornton walked around the room with her so Norah could speak with Judge Lee without interruption. She had no problem relating her feelings. She'd had plenty of practice trying to convince Thornton Winter.

The personal questioning, however, was quite blunt. Norah hoped the judge did not notice the blush she tried to hide when she was asked if she and Thornton had any romantic interest in each other. The discussion they had had the night he kissed her had put everything into perspective. Thank goodness, that was settled!

"We've settled that matter," Thornton said, echoing Norah's thoughts. "Miss Browne is quite young and needs friends her own age, while I have . . . a prior commitment."

"Do either of you plan to marry in the foreseeable future?" the judge asked, her eyebrows raised over her tortoise-shell glasses. She seemed satisfied when they responded in the negative.

Judge Lee explained why custody could not be permanent. Norah was new to the area and had her own adjustments to make. She might decide that Charleston was not where she wished to make her permanent residence. They were both single. Situations could change. If that occurred, the court should be notified immediately.

"Six months joint custody," the judge ruled, tapping her gavel lightly.

Norah paled as the papers were put in front of her. Camille's future would soon be a matter of a legal transaction. But it was only temporary custody. Norah signed.

"Let me hold the baby," Judge Lee said and took her from Thornton, who stepped up to the desk and placed his signature on the document.

When he looked up, Norah saw that his eyes were misty. He reached for Norah and held her close. "Thank you," he said and she knew he'd been right. They should be able to behave as good friends, and good friends hugged each other in times of emotional stress.

After the brief embrace, they moved away. Norah's eyes, too, wer wet.

"You're a lucky little girl," the judge crooned, and Camille grabbed her glasses. "Feisty, too."

Norah couldn't resist a parting word as she gathered up

Camille and her belongings to leave. "Takes after her uncle."

❧

They began making the move into the house on Meeting Street the following day, but would not complete the move until after the weekend. Norah had wanted the transition to be as smooth and natural as possible for Camille, so together they had decided that they would spend most weekends at the beach house, since the baby's swimming lessons were scheduled for Saturday.

Hilda, a tall, dark-skinned woman with a handsome face and flashing black eyes, moved into her rooms downstairs and set to work transforming the place.

Their first night in the townhouse, Hilda set a bowl in front of Norah. "Let's see how you like this," she said with a dare in her tone.

Norah dipped her soup spoon into the bowl and tasted. "Wonderful!" she proclaimed. With her second spoonful, she allowed a little to dribble down her chin, much to Hilda's delight. "I've never tasted anything like it. What is it?"

"She-crab soup," Hilda said proudly.

When she returned to the kitchen, Thornton leaned over and touched Norah's arm. "That was your initiation. I think she might let you stay."

Norah soon learned that Hilda had every right to be proud. She had more energy than three people, served delicious Southern fare that she insisted was reduced in fat and cholesterol, and kept the household running on a schedule, as much as possible with a baby in the house.

Thornton had Camille's Babyland furniture taken out of storage and shipped to the house. When Norah turned on the clown lamp, Camille stared at it curiously. She was restless that night, and Norah wondered if she might have some memory associated with the loss of her parents. So she held Camille longer than usual, even after she had finally drifted off to sleep.

Norah mentioned it to Thornton. After a thoughtful moment, he made a suggestion. "Perhaps we should have Eloise stop in a few days a week, so Camille won't feel she's lost another person she's grown close to."

Norah agreed, pleased with his sensitivity, and Aunt Tess, as busy as she was with her church work and garden club, also dropped in frequently for meals and visits. Thornton, too, rearranged his office schedule so he could spend time with Camille during her waking hours.

When he described the assistance Norah could give him in his work, she no longer doubted that it was a "real" job. He spent most of the day at his office, while she worked in the library at the house, researching, writing, editing, and recording information about homes and buildings he would renovate. Occasionally, she accompanied him on visits to potential clients. Once or twice, when they were working together, she noticed him shoving a pad of paper out of sight when she came near, as if it were something she shouldn't see. Probably one of those sketches "unfit for human eyes" when it was first started, she decided.

Norah's favorite time of day, though, was late evening, after she and Thornton had settled in the library to discuss some project or plan the next day's work. She loved hearing him talk about his plans and dreams and soon learned that renovation meant much more than a new room or a fresh coat of paint.

Thornton compared it with one's spiritual life. "It's like a rebirth, Norah," he explained, leaning back in his desk chair. "I gain satisfaction by taking something timeworn, faded, broken, and restoring its natural beauty. I love to make it useful again."

"You make renovation sound almost human," Norah mused aloud.

He smiled. "With people, the results are even more reward-ing."

"Then you should feel very rewarded," she said softly.

She might have been referring to his brothers. Or Camille. But Thornton suspected that Norah was talking about herself. He knew she badly needed the security, stability, and family life that he made possible for her. It was, indeed, gratifying to know that he had enabled her life to be fulfilled in so many ways.

Still, he tried not to think of time passing so quickly. It was like Judge Lee had said—too much was temporary, change-able. And he strongly feared that someone was going to be hurt. Deeply.

But for the moment, he would enjoy this newfound happi-ness. It was just a matter of time until he would be able to forgive both Lantz and Madelyn. He felt it happening. Life was too good, too busy, too full, to allow bitterness to thrive in his soul.

❧

Norah had grown to love the sound of the bells of St. Michael's pealing through the city on Sunday morning, to appreciate the look of the historic old churches she had once disdained. And one Sunday after services at the Mt. Pleasant church, where she was still attending with Josh, Thornton gave her a tour. Rather than stuffy, the mellow old building seemed worship-ful and beautiful with its ornate carvings, chancel decorations, high pulpit, cushioned foot rests, and box pews with hinged doors.

Filled with a new awareness of God's omnipresence—past, present, and future—she knew He was here just as fully as in Josh's church, though she still felt a need for the down-to-earthness of the simple people in Mt. Pleasant. It was her one activity separate and distinct from Thornton Winter's world, in which she had become so enmeshed.

Surprisingly, Thornton had relented, allowing her to take Camille to the church in Mt. Pleasant. He insisted upon driving them there and picking them up, however, although it was out of the way and his church was within walking distance of the house on Meeting Street.

"Make sure Josh or someone is with you, in case something happens to delay me," he warned.

It suddenly occurred to Norah that he might fear kidnapping. Camille was the child of celebrities and in the custody of a very prominent man. "Do you think it's safe?" she asked, disturbed.

"In Mt. Pleasant, at that church, yes," he said, "and Josh Logan has had an impeccable reputation for the past eight years."

"You had him checked out?"

"Aunt Tess retired from the College last year, remember?" he retorted.

As it turned out, Thornton was never late. It became a weekly ritual that the Rolls, which he kept in town, would appear in the parking lot promptly at the conclusion of the service, and he'd be standing against it in his conservative suit, with his arms folded across his chest.

The first Sunday, Norah wasn't surprised to see Aunt Tess in front, but was astounded to see Madelyn sitting in the back. And when she climbed in with Camille, Madelyn was unusually gracious to Norah and entranced with the baby, who waved her arms and gurgled, apparently intrigued with the bright red color of the designer creation Madelyn was wearing.

"She's so pretty," said Madelyn in her soft Southern drawl. "May . . . I touch her?"

Norah, who had never heard the woman speak more than two words, was startled, but nodded in agreement, then watched as Madelyn extended a long, graceful finger, tipped with a perfectly polished nail. Out of the corner of her eye, Norah saw Aunt Tess turn her head to peek around the front seat.

Madelyn had barely touched the velvety skin before Camille grabbed her pearl bracelet.

"Uh, oh! We wouldn't want to get those in your mouth," Norah said gently. She unfastened the tiny hands. But Camille didn't want to be unfastened and wailed as if someone had struck her.

"Oh, I'm so sorry!" Madelyn said, shrinking back against the seat. There was a shadow in the blue eyes, and her lips trembled.

"It's not your fault," Norah said quickly. "All babies try to put things in their mouths. Here, hold up your arm."

Madelyn obeyed reluctantly.

"Now, Camille, touch the pretty bracelet ea—sy," Norah said, guiding her hand. "Ea—sy." The wailing stopped and Camille began to enjoy the game.

Madelyn's expression softened. The look in her eyes was lovely and adoring, and Norah knew that, unless Madelyn was a schizophrenic, she was innately a very gentle person.

For an instant, Norah felt some unnamed dread, and her eyes met Thornton's in the rearview mirror. He quickly shifted his gaze to the road, and a muscle in his face twitched as his jaw tightened.

What it all meant, Norah didn't know. But the routine persisted. Each Sunday, Madelyn came home with them and stayed for Hilda's fabulous dinner and a leisurely visit afterward. And each week, within the nurturing family circle, and with the innocent baby to focus their attention upon, Madelyn opened up just a little more, blossoming like a lovely flower before their eyes.

One day soon after a particularly pleasant Sunday afternoon, Thornton said to Norah, "I think it's time you got to know Madelyn."

Norah was puzzled. "But I already know her."

"I am speaking as your employer now. The McCallas have decided to renovate. I need you to do research, make notes, take measurements, that kind of thing. We need to know the personalities of all the people in the home in order to do the job justice."

Much to Norah's surprise, she found the McCallas to be a charming couple, whose heritage was as impressive as Thornton's. Their home was an antebellum plantation home, surrounded by huge old oaks. More surprising was Madelyn's overture of friendship.

"I'm sorry I behaved so badly when we first met," she confided, telling Norah that she had been in love with Thornton, then Lantz, and had been at the Winter house when Lantz broke off the relationship. She had been devastated. Thornton had returned home while the argument was taking place and had seen Madelyn run outside and jump into her car. He had followed and had managed to climb in before she roared off.

"I wanted to die," Madelyn explained in a whispery voice, "so I didn't even notice the storm or the rain-soaked roads. I just pushed the gas pedal to the floorboard. Thorn tried to stop me, but the car' planed and left the road. It hit an embankment and overturned."

Madelyn put her hands over her face, and Norah had to strain to hear her next words. "The air bag protected me, but the passenger's side wasn't protected. His face . . . was full of glass and metal."

Madelyn couldn't talk any more that day, but on Norah's second visit, she learned that, after she'd seen the damage to Thornton's face, Madelyn had taken an overdose of sleeping pills and had been under a doctor's care ever since, recuperating in the home of relatives in Paris.

"Every time I look at him, I could just die," she groaned. Tears of guilt and remorse slid down her beautiful face. "Thornton has helped me with the guilt. He says he's forgiven me." There was a haunted look in the beautiful eyes. "But how can a person forgive someone for ruining his life?"

Though Norah didn't say so, she was more concerned about what Madelyn had done to his heart. And a few weeks later, she discovered that Madelyn, too, was not insensitive to that aspect of their relationship.

Madelyn's parents had dropped her off at the house with some written suggestions concerning the renovation. While she talked with Thornton in the library, Norah went upstairs to read for a while. Later, she decided to go down and see if Thornton was ready to discuss the instructions with her.

Seeing a faint light from the living room and hearing the sound of voices, Norah paused. *Madelyn must still be here.* Nearing the room, Norah froze and stepped back into the shadows. Through the gap in the partially opened door, she could see the two of them standing very close together. Madelyn was gazing up into Thornton's face.

"I made a terrible mistake, Thorn," she was saying. "I'm so sorry. It's you I love. I've *always* loved you."

"We'll talk about it later, Madelyn," Thornton said gently. "We'll go to dinner tomorrow night and discuss it then."

Norah couldn't bear to hear any more, but turned and fled back up the stairs. She shouldn't have listened, shouldn't have watched. She didn't want to admit that Madelyn had become a very likable person—now that Thornton was . . . restoring her.

❧

Time was passing quickly. Before long, the end of the six-month period would be upon them. Norah had tried to establish a life of her own. She'd really tried. Sometimes she went to lunch with Josh, to youth outings, or an occasional dinner. Theirs was a good, solid friendship. He needed to talk about his murdered sister as much as she needed to talk about her life in the Winter household. And without discussing it, Josh knew how she felt about Thornton Winter. She'd miss their talks when he left at the end of the summer.

It was during the weekend of July fourth, which they celebrated at the beach house, that Thornton and Norah decided to throw a party for Camille's six-month birthday during the third week in July. Norah added that she would also like to give a going-away party for Josh, who would be returning to North Carolina in August. They decided to combine the two and invite only family and a few close friends.

Norah asked the young couple who ran the church nursery. Aunt Tess invited the dean of the college. Chris brought a young couple and a pretty girl named Jennifer. Madelyn was there, of course, with her parents. But the big surprise was the young pastor of Thornton's church, who came with his wife and their two small children. Their youth and friendliness belied Norah's old conviction that historic churches must surely have equally stuffy pastors.

It was a casual afternoon affair, and no one was dressed up . . . except for the guest of honor. Camille was adorable in a new yellow dress, compliments of Norah, and her black Mary Janes.

There were gifts galore—a battery-run Sesame Street train set from Thornton, a five-foot inflatable dragon from Chris, and an adorable music box that played "Jesus Loves Me" from Josh among others. But Camille wasn't about to be confined to her new walker, a gift from Aunt Tess, and insisted on being passed from one adult to another.

Norah was busy snapping pictures all afternoon—the guests, the birthday girl, the cake. She even got one of Josh leading them all in a rousing rendition of "Happy Birthday" as they gathered around the table.

It was after cake and ice cream that Mrs. McCalla asked to hold Camille. The baby loved all the attention and sat on Mrs. McCalla's lap while Mr. McCalla entertained her with a stuffed, talking Mickey Mouse. Madelyn knelt in front of them, her eyes shining. Mrs. McCalla glanced over at Thornton and said wistfully, "Oh, I've wanted grandchildren for so long."

The four of them made a touching little tableau, Norah realized, suddenly feeling out of place. She took the picture reluctantly.

Feeling her gaze on him, Thornton looked up and sensed her distress, but wasn't sure of its source. Then he watched as Josh observed it, too.

"Let's all pitch in and clear this mess so we can start the games. You have to have games at a party," he said loudly with a huge grin.

Soon, he had everyone involved in silly relay games, laughing and completely enjoying themselves. Thornton held Camille, who chortled in delight at the scene. But the afternoon's excitment was taking its toll.

After the guests had gone, Norah got the cranky baby settled for her nap while Thornton talked to Josh about his home and family in North Carolina and his plans for the future.

Later, Josh and Norah walked down to the beach. When they returned, Eloise made a light supper, Thornton declining Norah's invitation to eat with them on the deck.

Instead, he looked in on Camille, who was sleeping peacefully. Eloise had gone to her room. With no one to talk to, he returned to the game room. All the birthday wrappings had been picked up and the new toys stacked neatly. A glance through the windows told him it was getting dark, but he decided against turning on the deck lights.

Outside, Norah and Josh sat on the unlighted deck, while Norah tried to tell him how much she valued his friendship.

"It's mutual, Norah," Josh returned. "I think God knew you needed somebody by your side, and I needed someone to talk to about my sister. Nobody mentions her anymore at home. So thank you. And remember, we're friends. That means . . .

from now on!"

He stood, took her hands and began to sing, softly at first, then filling the night air with his rich baritone.

At first, Thornton thought someone had turned on the radio. Glancing out the window, he saw Norah and Josh standing very close together, their hands entwined. When Josh finished his song, their arms went around each other, and Thornton turned away, climbed the stairs, and sat on his deck for a very long time.

He knew when they drove to the dock, and he knew when Norah returned alone a few minutes later. Coming downstairs, he met her as she was coming into the house.

"I wanted you to know that my surgery—the reconstructive surgery for my face—is scheduled for next week, Norah."

Norah gasped. He hadn't mentioned it in ages.

He touched the raised scars. "The doctors said the scars would contract. That's why the skin is pulled and tight. It's meticulous work, of course, but relatively simple. We don't expect any problems."

She knew better, even as she asked the question. "Do you want me to go with you?"

"Thank you, but that won't be necessary." He added quickly, "Madelyn will be going with me. She feels a need to be there."

Norah's heart wrenched. *And what do you think I feel?*

He stood there, running his finger over the ridges in his face. She knew he had something else on his mind. "You're taking it well," he said at last.

"Well, you just told me the operation will be relatively simple."

"I was speaking of Josh's leaving."

She nodded, feeling the loss already. "I'll miss him," she admitted. "He's leaving one day next week, but I don't think we'll see each other again. Camille and I will go to your church Sunday." She looked down. "That is . . . if you still want us to."

At one time Thornton would have been overjoyed with that announcement. Now there was another pressing matter on his mind. "We'll talk tomorrow. Good night."

"Good night," Norah whispered, staring at the empty space where he had been long after he had left to go down the hall-way toward his room.

He would have his surgery. Madelyn would be with him. What more was there to say?

twelve

The next day there was not a breath of breeze stirring. The sun was a blazing ball in the sky, and there had been no cooling shower for over a week. Camille was especially fussy, and Norah awoke with a dull headache.

"I don't feel like going to church," she told Thornton. "And since Camille hasn't been to the nursery at your church, I'll keep her here with me."

Norah did look peaked, as if she hadn't slept well. Thornton nodded in concern. "Then get some rest. We'll be back for lunch."

Only Thornton and Madelyn came, as Aunt Tess had plans to visit a friend in the hospital. But Norah didn't feel much like joining them at the table, not with Madelyn looking cool and beautiful in white and gold, glowing like a frosty light bulb.

As the afternoon sun made its descent, the air cooled a little. But still no breeze stirred. Norah thought she and Camille might be more comfortable outside and took her to the far end of the deck, beyond the pool in the shade of the trees.

The walker was new to Camille and, for a while, she played with the colored wooden rings along the tray. Soon she was distracted by the other toys Norah placed on the tray and made a game of tossing them on the deck for Norah to retrieve. Each time Norah bent over, however, she felt the throbbing in her head and became freshly irritated with Thornton. By the time he and Madelyn finally strolled into view from far down the island, she was thoroughly put out with him.

Leaving Madelyn under the shade of a flowering shrub in

154

the garden, Thornton walked up to Norah. "Feeling better?"

"No."

"Anything I can do?"

"You can pick up the toys when Camille drops them. My head is splitting."

He pulled a chair close. "Norah, I'm sorry. I thought you wanted to be left alone."

"I do," she said, feeling the threat of tears. She mustn't cry.

"It's Josh, isn't it?"

A gasp raked her throat. Of course, that was part of it. "Not entirely," she said. "It's just an off day. Everyone has them. It's hot, and I have a headache."

Thornton kept leaning down to pick up the toys Camille was throwing. She was fretful. She'd be crying soon. "You need some help. I'll get Eloise."

"No," Norah said. "When the baby's fussy, she needs a *parent*." Norah regretted the look of guilt that crossed his face at her implication. She knew she was being unfair. But she felt so miserable.

"Norah, there's something I've been needing to say to you. . . ."

She'd been expecting this. But she couldn't bear to hear it. Not now.

"Madelyn's fragile, Norah, not strong like you." Now that he'd begun, the words came quickly. "She's been so filled with guilt. She couldn't believe that God and I could forgive her. It hasn't been easy to make her believe it."

It was all she could do to endure the excitement in his eyes as he proclaimed Madelyn's virtues. "She's begun to emerge as a whole person, now that she's ridding herself of guilt. She's becoming the woman she used to be—loving, gracious . . ."

"Good for her!" snapped Norah, seeing a white vision approach from the other side of the pool. Feeling as if the top of her head were about to explode, she jumped up, rammed her toe into the walker, and half hobbled, half ran toward a cluster of trees.

Camille was making whining, engine-revving noises.

But Thornton wasn't through. It had to be now, or he could never go through with it. He followed her to the shady spot where she clung weakly to a palm. "There's more I need to say, Norah."

"I don't want to hear it," she protested. If he said another word, she'd scream.

But the scream didn't come from Norah.

The sound pierced the air like some high-pitched signal of disaster. Loud and long and frantic. Norah and Thornton turned. They saw it all in one blinding flash. They ran, but it was too late. The scene had already been set. As if in slow motion, they could see the bright-colored ball rolling into the pool, floating temptingly on the surface, Camille in hot pursuit, her red ringlets bobbing up and down, the walker picking up speed by the second, while the baby's arms and legs pumped wildly.

Eloise, seeing the impending disaster from the glass doors, could only scream helplessly and run back in to dial the emergency number.

Norah and Thornton ran, but it seemed as if their legs were weighted, as in some awful nightmare. As soon as the front wheels left the poolside, the walker tipped over, dislodging the baby and plunging her into the water head first, then toppling in on top of her.

For one horrifying moment, they lost sight of Camille. Her ball bobbed innocently nearby, reflecting the dazzling sunlight. Had she already hurtled to the bottom? Was she trapped beneath the walker?

Norah was right behind Thornton, who plunged in, shoes and all. Then they were all in the pool. Madelyn reached the screaming baby first, lifting Camille over her head, then going down with her mouth and eyes wide open in frozen terror.

Norah grabbed the baby and Thornton dove for Madelyn. Before Norah could reach the side of the pool, she realized that Camille was gurgling happily, splashing the water with her hands and feet. The baby seemed happier than she had all day, delighted with her impromptu diving lesson.

Eloise ran out and took the soggy child from Norah. "I'll check her over," she said. "I called an ambulance and the pediatrician."

Looking around, Norah saw Thornton struggling to roll a limp Madelyn over the side of the pool and swam over to help.

The sound of sirens announced the arrival of the EMT's, but Thornton had already revived Madelyn by the time they got to the pool with their stretcher. He wrapped his arm around her shoulders while she coughed and gagged and spit up water. Then unmindful of their bedraggled condition, her lovely white dress plastered against her body, Thornton held her, rocking back and forth, while she sobbed out her relief.

Feeling drippy and drained, Norah hurried inside to be with Camille, who was proclaimed none the worse for her ordeal by the pediatrician. By nightfall, however, she had a slight fever, diagnosed as a virus, and was put to bed early.

By the next day, Camille was her bright little self again. Norah, on the other hand, was ill with flu-like symptoms and felt sick enough to die. She deserved to, she knew. What if Camille had not been thrown out of the walker? What if Madelyn hadn't been there? What if . . .?

On Sunday night they moved back to the town house, and Thornton drove Madelyn back to the McCallas. On Monday he was back, along with Aunt Tess, Hilda, and Eloise. Norah could eat nothing and, when anyone looked in on her to see what she might need, she shook her head, put her hands over her face, and dissolved into fresh tears.

By Tuesday morning her fever was gone and her throat felt better, but she was reluctant to hold Camille, though she longed to cuddle her close.

"What you need is some nourishment, Miss Norah," Hilda declared, propping the pillows behind her head. "You need to get your strength back." She left to prepare her famous milk toast.

But it was Thornton who brought in the tray. Norah nervously ran her fingers through her uncombed hair. She must look awful. "Feeling better?" he asked as cheerfully as he could manage. She glanced at him, and the waterworks started again.

He set the tray on the bedside table and sat on the edge of her bed. "I know," he said. "You must feel like I do." His swimming eyes overflowed.

"It's my fault," she choked out.

"No more than mine," he insisted.

"Madelyn saved her life, Thornton. I shudder to think . . ."

"Madelyn can't even swim, Norah," he said incredulously.

Norah's tears halted. "Wh—what?"

He nodded. "Her younger sister drowned in a swimming pool when Madelyn was four. She saw it happen and ran to tell her mother. It's her earliest memory and she's been deathly afraid of water ever since."

"She . . . risked her life," Norah breathed in amazement, "while I was . . . thinking about myself. Oh, Thornton . . ."

"No," he soothed, laying a comforting hand over her clenched fists. "We were *both* supposed to be watching Camille. You have to forgive yourself, as I have to forgive myself. We made a mistake, Norah, but we musn't punish ourselves like Madelyn has done. . . ."

Madelyn! "I must thank her," she said, struggling to sit up.

"Later." He handed her a glass of orange juice. "As terrible as this was, Norah, it's a major turning point for Madelyn.

For so long she's felt completely worthless and punished herself for what she did to me."

Norah lifted the glass to her lips and sipped slowly. In the past few hours, Madelyn had made up for everything, she thought. She could never again have an unkind or jealous thought about the woman.

"Norah," he said softly when the tears again rained down her cheeks, "you're the one who thought of the swimming lessons, remember?"

Sniffing, she nodded. "And you gave your permission." She tried to smile.

"I'm having dinner with the McCallas, but Madelyn and I will stop by afterwards, Norah." He walked to the door. "I'll see you right before I leave."

Norah grasped the glass with both hands, but they were still trembling. Madelyn, not she, would help Thornton through his operation. But she mustn't think of herself. That kind of self-absorption had already proven to be disastrous.

৵

They arrived shortly before seven. Norah and Aunt Tess were sitting in the parlor beneath the ceiling fan, drinking cool glasses of lemonade when Thornton and Madelyn rushed in.

"I drove over here!" Madelyn reported excitedly. "It's the first time since the accident. I didn't think I would ever drive again, but Thornton said it was time." The adoring look she gave him chilled Norah's heart.

But she set her glass down and walked over to embrace Madelyn. "Of course you can. There isn't anything in the world you can't do . . . now." Her voice caught and Madelyn smiled like an angel. "Thank you sounds so inadequate. . . ."

"You would have done the same," Madelyn said graciously.

"Yes," Norah agreed. "But I *didn't*. You *did*."

"I'm just glad I was there," Madelyn said, her face radiant. "May I see Camille before we leave?"

"Of course."

"I'll go up with you," said Aunt Tess and followed Madelyn toward the stairs.

"She's different," Norah told Thornton when the two women had left. "I think it's confidence."

She was also pretty sure it was love. But no matter what, Norah could no longer believe that Madelyn would not be good for Thornton. She was an extraordinary woman.

"Let's go in the library," Thornton said gently.

She turned to him in astonishment, but he was already walking toward the door. *How could she face him in the room where he had kissed her? But then again, perhaps it was the most appropriate place for him to tell her of his love for another woman. If she cried, she could always blame it on her guilt over Camille's accident.*

The drapes had been kept closed to block out the sun since there was still no relief from the heat. Thornton flipped a switch at the doorway, and the fan in the center of the high ceiling began to revolve. Norah was glad he hadn't turned on the light. It would be easier if the room remained dim and shadowy.

She sat down in the same chair she'd sat in that other night and held onto the arms. That was silly, she told herself, and put her hands in her lap. When a tornado strikes full force, there is really nothing much one can do. Why didn't he just go ahead and say he and Madelyn were going to be married?

Thornton stood behind the opposite chair and held onto the back, watching her carefully as he said, "After the surgery, Norah, Madelyn and I will be leaving for Paris."

He'd thought she might rage at him, condemn him for going away so soon after Camille's mishap . . . maybe even beg him to stay. But she made no demands, no accusation, no indication that it mattered. Regardless of his feelings, he had to do what seemed right. "If you want to leave . . . with Josh . . . I won't try to stop you." Her eyes flew to his, so he quickly added, "With Camille, of course. The two of you could make a good life for her. Josh is a good man. I've watched him. I'm convinced he would make a fine father."

Norah couldn't believe her ears. Something—the whirring of the fan or her medication—was making her senses whirl. She rubbed a hand across her forehead.

"Norah," he said with difficulty, "I mean it. You don't have to wait until the six months are up. I can't bring myself to separate you from the child you love like a mother, and I will not keep you from Josh if he's the man you love."

If she told him she didn't love Josh, would Thornton do the noble thing and not marry Madelyn? It seemed highly unlikely. And with Madelyn's act of selfless heroism, any idea of competing with her for Thornton's heart had been laid to rest forever.

"I can't believe this," Norah said, still unable to take it all in.

"Neither can I," he said. "At least I couldn't until the accident."

So that's when he had made his final decision, Norah thought, as he came around the chair and slumped into it. *That's when he knew how much Madelyn meant to him. After all, she had almost died in that pool.*

Thornton leaned forward, resting his forearms on his thighs, his head down, staring at the floor. "Norah, losing several people I've loved has taught me some hard lessons. We instinctively want to hold our loved ones close, guard them jealously. But the deepest kind of love means being willing to let them go, if it's for the best." He lifted his head and looked at her. "I want you to know that putting aside my own feelings in this is the hardest thing I've ever done." He glanced toward the doorway, and the light from the parlor glinted in his eyes, revealing the anguish in them.

Norah had to clasp her hands together to keep from reaching out, begging him not to do this wonderful, terrible thing. But she, too, could not listen to her own heart. *If he and Madelyn could find happiness together, she mustn't interfere.* Hot tears stained her face.

Thornton took another step. He seemed reluctant to go, his hand lingering on the curve of her chair back. "I'll set up a trust for Camille. We'll want to visit, of course, from time to time." Eternity passed before he could speak again. "Leave some pictures for me . . . of *both* of you."

She tried to speak but no words would come. All she could do was close her eyes and shake her head.

"I know it will take time for you to absorb this." She heard the starkness in his voice and her shoulders began to shake with her silent sobs. "Kiss Camille goodbye for me. I won't see her. I don't want her to sense this emptiness I already feel."

Norah sat there long after he had gone, oblivious to the whispered voices around her, the soft footsteps of people coming and going to check on her. At last she roused, her gaze falling upon the empty picture frame on the desk. *It would be filled, and her heart would be empty.* With an ache worse than the flu, she left the room.

❧

On Wednesday morning, Norah strolled Camille along the sidewalk, speaking to neighbors and friendly strangers on the street. She went into Thornton's silent church, regretting that she hadn't attended services there with him. "Show me the right thing to do," she prayed, and dreaded what the answer might be.

The hours she spent with Camille seemed more precious than ever. So did the house she'd been reluctant to move into. Now that she dreaded leaving, she must. Over and over, she kept reminding herself to think only of what was best for the child.

That evening, Thornton called. Norah didn't want to talk to him, so Aunt Tess took the call. "No," she said and turned away so Norah could not hear her whispered conversation. Suspecting that they were speaking about her, Norah left the room.

When she returned Aunt Tess insisted on staying overnight. "The surgery was a long, drawn-out procedure," she reported, "but it was successful, Thornton says." She eyed Norah carefully before adding, "They'll leave for Paris tonight."

By Thursday, Norah knew she must get on with her life. There were options, she told herself. She could return to California and live with her parents until she finished school, then find a job.

And if she could believe Thornton who had told her she was young and beautiful, she thought with a wry smile, she should be able to find a dozen men who'd fall in love with her. She could have children. Life wasn't over, she told herself, but the tears kept falling, like a southern rainstorm.

Or she might even go to North Carolina and take Psychology under Josh Logan. He'd said he had a family who even took in stray cats. Josh was a friend. He could help. To a point. She could love him as a friend, but now that Thornton Winter had so invaded her life, her senses, her emotions, she knew there could never be another man who moved her so.

Maybe Thornton knew she loved him. Maybe he'd deliberately tried to influence her thinking by reminding her that when you truly love someone, you do what's best for them. Whatever his reasons, she would try and act upon what she felt was best for Camille.

Writing the letter was the hardest thing yet. "Dear Thornton," she began, then crumpled the page into a tight ball.

Taking a fresh sheet, she started over. She must forget the familiarity. She must think of him as Mr. Winter, the

Southern gentleman who'd graciously taken her in, who could give Camille everything she would ever need, including his love   . . . and a lovely, gentle woman for a mommy.

"But she can't love you like I do," Norah said aloud, feeling the suffocating grief. With an aching throat and hot, burning eyes, she wrote down all the things she wanted him to know, but had never dared to say. Then she threw the letter away. Some things were better left unsaid.

After playing with Camille for the last time, she scribbled a note:

> *Thornton,*
>
> *I know you will take good care of Camille. If you need any papers signed, contact my parents. And please send me a picture or a note some-time. Tell her about her aunt, who will love her always . . .*

She paused, then rewrote the note, striking out the last sentence. She'd have to trust Thornton and Madelyn to tell Camille about her in their own way. She wrote a few more lines, almost adding, "Be happy," but that seemed redundant. Instead, she wrote, "God bless you all," and signed her name, "Norah Browne."

Norah called Aunt Tess, who came right over after hearing the distress in her voice. Her bags were already in the Mercedes. "I'm leaving," she said as soon as Aunt Tess stepped inside.

"Now?" Aunt Tess asked, a puzzled look on her face. "Thornton said you and Josh would be taking Camille before he returns, but I didn't know it would be this soon. I'm so sorry it had to be this way, dear, but I understand and hope you'll bring her back to see us often."

"I'm not going with Josh, and I'm not taking Camille, Aunt Tess. I'm leaving her for Thornton and Madelyn." At Aunt Tess' bewildered look, the tears Norah had tried to suppress spilled over.

"Does Thornton know?" At the shake of Norah's head, Tess was alarmed. "Oh, honey," she begged, "do wait till he comes back."

"I can't," Norah sobbed brokenly. "The baby's sleeping now. But if she wakes up and sees me . . . I might not be able to go through with this."

Tess patted her shoulder. "Don't worry about a thing. We'll take good care of her. But oh, how we'll miss you, my dear!"

With that, Norah fell into Aunt Tess' arms and sobbed out her pain. Then stumbling down the steps, she climbed into the car and drove away.

Tess stood watching until the Mercedes had disappeared around a corner. "I don't understand," she said, not comprehending. Then, as the truth dawned, her face lit up. "Of course I do!"

▪

An hour later, Norah arrived at the dock. Henry was bending over the engine of her Rabbit with a screwdriver in his oily hand.

"Don't know what's the matter with it," he said, unwinding his tall frame and scratching his head. "Can't get it started. I've been trying to keep all the cars running, but when one of them sits here for weeks . . ."

"Let me try," she said. "It's been temperamental for years, but I thought it was fixed."

She got in and turned the ignition key, but the maneuvers she'd tried in the past failed to start the engine.

"Maybe I could jump-start it. I'll need a special kind of cable, though. I'll run home and see if I can find it. I can call you down at the house when it's ready."

She drove to the beach house to wait for Henry's call. Eloise was there.

Thirty minutes later, Chris arrived.

"What are *you* doing here?" she asked.

"Well," he began, but before he could finish, in came Aunt Tess with Camille.

"What's going on?" she asked, bewildered.

"I talked to Thornton," Aunt Tess said. "He said to tell you not to do anything foolish, because you're not going anywhere . . . with or without this baby."

"Wh—what . . . did he mean?" she stammered.

"I don't know. He didn't have time to talk, but said he'd be here just as soon as possible."

Norah wondered if Madelyn would be coming with him. Of course she would. She was his wife, wasn't she? Or soon would be.

∞

Dark clouds started rolling in the following morning, and the wind picked up, bringing some relief from the blistering heat. A storm seemed imminent, a common occurrence for the last of July, Aunt Tess said, a prelude to the hurricane season when it wouldn't be sensible to stay at the beach house.

Thornton called from the airport to say he was on his way, so Eloise started supper. Norah knew she wouldn't be able to eat a bite. To help pass the time, the family engaged her in trivial conversation. The next call was from the dock. He was only minutes away.

Norah walked over to the sliding glass doors, standing like a statue, trying to convince herself that it was not her heart that was pounding so loudly, but thunder. The darkness that had enveloped the world outside those doors was but a foreshadowing of what she must endure when she'd see Madelyn hanging on his arm.

She remembered something Josh had said. When all else

fails, try the prayer of serenity. Well, she was helpless to change
the situation. She must accept it. And she had prayed for
God's will to be done, not her own. Now she had to put herself aside and recommit herself to Camille's best interests. It
was not best to divide that child nor to drag her through end-
less court battles if she could have two loving parents. If ever
she had needed strength beyond her own, Norah thought, it
was now.

The deck lights hadn't yet been turned on, and the sky had
darkened to black. The glass doors mirrored the little group
inside—Eloise puttering in the kitchen, Aunt Tess sitting on a
bar stool, talking to Norah, Chris playing with Camille on a
quilt in the middle of the floor.

Suddenly, the door slid aside, and Thornton burst into the
room, apparently blown there by the wind that lifted his black
curls above the silver at his temples. A small bandage covered the area next to his eye, but the skin was no longer taut.
The eye was normal—beautiful, black, gleaming, fixed on
Norah. Maybe Madelyn wouldn't cry now when she looked
at him.

The scar that zigzagged down his cheek deepened in color
and Norah knew he was upset with her. Why? Did he feel he
had to return from a rendezvous with Madelyn—their honey-
moon?—in order to take care of the baby? And where was
Madelyn? Had he let her out at the front so she could come
through the house?

Thornton didn't wait for Norah to comment on his face. He
would be more acceptable to some people now, but he knew it
had never mattered to her. Aunt Tess had read him the note
Norah had pinned to her pillow. The note had stated that she
was not leaving with Josh and that she would not be taking
Camille. What could that mean? If she didn't love Josh,
then . . .

Camille cried out as Thornton closed the door behind him.

He hurried over to her, concerned.

"I think she wants to go swimming," Chris said, laughing. "When you came in and the wind hit her face, she held her breath."

Norah watched as Thornton picked up the baby, held her close in his arms, rocking her until she quieted while the rest of the family gathered around to comment on his surgery.

"Is Madelyn all right?" Aunt Tess asked, echoing Norah's unspoken question.

"I think she's finally convinced that she doesn't owe me her life, that she should forget the past and make a new start," Thornton said. "She had just begun to do that in Paris, before she returned here to all the memories." He paused. "That now leaves me free to make something permanent out of all this 'temporary' situation with a beautiful green-eyed redhead."

Norah's eyes met his over Camille's head, and her heart stopped. So Aunt Tess had told him about the note. "But Camille's eyes are blue," she said foolishly.

"Exactly," he said and handed the baby to Aunt Tess, who said she thought it would be a good idea if they were to check the house and make sure all the windows were closed. Eloise muttered something about supper being ruined, but better that than a couple of lives, and she left to tend to something on the stove. Chris grinned at his brother and followed the others down the hallway, pulling the string of the talking Mickey Mouse.

The wind whistled and rattled the glass doors, while the thunder clapped. Lightning flashed, revealing billowing dark clouds against a silver background.

Too long, Thornton thought, he'd been like an ocean wave, bravely approaching the shore, then losing power and timidly retreating back into the sea. He wouldn't make that mistake again. He would reach out for what he wanted so much.

In one long stride, he was facing Norah, no longer trying to hide anything from her. It was time for complete honesty. "Do you love Josh?" He had to hear it for himself.

"Only as a friend," she murmured.

"Then why do you want to leave me?" He just couldn't understand her.

"Oh, I'd never leave you if I thought you wanted me to stay. I thought you and Madelyn would be married by now. And I couldn't possibly live in the house with you and . . . a wife because . . ."

"Because?" he asked softly. Warmth and expectation sparked his eyes.

"Because I love you," she said simply. "And don't tell me not to! And this is what I think of your new face."

She moved nearer and drew his head down to hers. She kissed his scarred cheek as she had done that other night. But it was not the wound on his face she had touched and healed over the past months. It was his heart.

He felt like the seagull that had spread its wings and taken flight. "Norah," he whispered, "you began to change my life from the first moment I met you. But I'd rather give you up than have you stay with me out of a sense of obligation to Camille."

His arms came around her. The green glow of her eyes was as soft as her lips as she asked wistfully, "You love me, Thornton?"

"More than I ever thought possible. It seemed too wonderful to believe, too unreasonable, that you might love me, too. I even started sketches of the kind of home you might like. You've created a storm in my life, Norah—powerful and beautiful and cleansing. I feel alive again."

"Oh, Thornton," she breathed, "I've felt so desolate, thinking I would lose both you and Camille."

He held her close. "That was your last chance, Norah. You'll never get away from me now. I want to marry you and fight with you every day for the rest of our lives."

She drew back and cocked her head. "Fight?"

He grinned. "Don't you always do the opposite of whatever I say?"

Her love for him shone through the green gaze. "I'd much rather make up."

"Delighted to oblige." He bent over her lips in a lingering kiss of promise and commitment. "It's the only gentlemanly thing to do."

A Letter To Our Readers

Dear Reader:

In order that we might better contribute to your reading enjoyment, we would appreciate your taking a few minutes to respond to the following questions. When completed, please return to the following:

Rebecca Germany, Editor
Heartsong Presents
P.O. Box 719
Uhrichsville, Ohio 44683

1. Did you enjoy reading *Southern Gentleman*?
   ☐ Very much. I would like to see more books
      by this author!
   ☐ Moderately
      I would have enjoyed it more if _____

   _____

2. Are you a member of *Heartsong Presents*? Yes No
   If no, where did you purchase this book? _____

   _____

3. What influenced your decision to purchase
   this book? (Circle those that apply.)

Cover	Back cover copy
Title	Friends
Publicity	Other _____

4. On a scale from 1 (poor) to 10 (superior), please rate the following elements.

    ___Heroine   ___Plot

    ___Hero   ___Inspirational theme

    ___Setting   ___Secondary characters

5. What settings would you like to see covered in *Heartsong Presents* books?

_____

_____

6. What are some inspirational themes you would like to see treated in future books?_____

_____

_____

7. Would you be interested in reading other *Heartsong Presents* titles?   Yes   No

8. Please circle your age range:

| Under 18 | 18-24 | 25-34 |
| 35-45 | 46-55 | Over 55 |

9. How many hours per week do you read? _____

Name _____

Occupation _____

Address _____

City _____ State _____ Zip _____

Norma Jean Lutz

___Fields of Sweet Content___—When Alecia is summoned to Oklahoma by her sister, she never expected to be in the classroom again, as well as, become the key to unlock the prison of sorrow surrounding a father and his daughter. HP41 $2.95.

___Love's Silken Melody___—Roshelle Ramone is a star, yet deep, hidden memories and feelings of guilt continue to haunt and paralyze her. Even Victor Moran, the handsome recording company owner, who truly loves her, cannot reach past the darkness of Rochelle's past. HP57 $2.95.

*Look for *Cater to a Whim,* the newest book by Norma Jean Lutz, coming to you soon from *Heartsong Presents*.

....Hearts ♥ ong....

······ Presents ········

Great Inspirational Romance at a Great Price!

Heartsong Presents books are inspirational romances in contemporary and historical settings, designed to give you an enjoyable, spirit-lifting reading experience. You can choose from 84 wonderfully written titles from some of today's best authors like Colleen L. Reece, Brenda Bancroft, Janelle Jamison, and many others.

When ordering quantities less than twelve, above titles are $2.95 each.

SEND TO: Heartsong Presents Reader's Service
         P.O. Box 719, Uhrichsville, Ohio 44683

Please send me the items checked above. I am enclosing $ _____
(please add $1.00 to cover postage per order. OH add 6.5% tax. PA and NJ add 6%.). Send check or money order, no cash or C.O.D.s, please.
To place a credit card order, call 1-800-847-8270.

NAME _____

ADDRESS _____

CITY/STATE_____ ZIP _____

LOVE A GREAT LOVE STORY?

Introducing Heartsong Presents —
                              Your Inspirational Book Club

Heartsong Presents Christian romance reader's service will provide you with four never before published romance titles every month! In fact, your books will be mailed to you at the same time advance copies are sent to book reviewers. You'll preview each of these new and unabridged books before they are released to the general public.

These books are filled with the kind of stories you have been longing for—stories of courtship, chivalry, honor, and virtue. Strong characters and riveting plot lines will make you want to read on and on. Romance is not dead, and each of these romantic tales will remind you that Christian faith is still the vital ingredient in an intimate relationship filled with true love and honest devotion.

Sign up today to receive your first set. Send no money now. We'll bill you only $9.97 post-paid with your shipment. Then every month you'll automatically receive the latest four "hot off the press" titles for the same low post-paid price of $9.97. That's a savings of 50% off the $4.95 cover price. When you consider the exaggerated shipping charges of other book clubs, your savings are even greater!

THERE IS NO RISK—you may cancel at any time without obligation. And if you aren't completely satisfied with any selection, return it for an immediate refund.

TO JOIN, just complete the coupon below, mail it today, and get ready for hours of wholesome entertainment.

Now you can curl up, relax, and enjoy some great reading full of the warmhearted spirit of romance.